Praise for *Merlin's Harp*

"The story glows. . . . A bounty of original poems
and legends enhances the narrative
considerably. In creating a mythical tapestry that
is at once completely recognizable yet utterly
fresh, Crompton has spun a worthy successor to
the weavings of T. H. White."
—*Publishers Weekly*

"Lyrical. . . . Crompton's flowing prose creates an
atmosphere in which the familiar tale becomes
fresh again."
—*Library Journal*

"Crompton spins a good yarn."
—*Chicago Tribune*

"Its strengths lie in its poetic language and its
finely wrought spiritual sense. A riveting
good read."
—*Booklist*

PERCIVAL'S ANGEL

Anne Eliot
Crompton

A ROC BOOK

ROC
Published by New American Library, a division of
Penguin Putnam Inc., 375 Hudson Street,
New York, New York 10014, U.S.A.
Penguin Books Ltd, 27 Wrights Lane,
London W8 5TZ, England
Penguin Books Australia Ltd, Ringwood,
Victoria, Australia
Penguin Books Canada Ltd, 10 Alcorn Avenue,
Toronto, Ontario, Canada M4V 3B2
Penguin Books (N.Z.) Ltd, 182–190 Wairau Road,
Auckland 10, New Zealand

Penguin Books Ltd, Registered Offices:
Harmondsworth, Middlesex, England

First published by Roc, an imprint of New American Library, a division of
Penguin Putnam Inc.

First Printing, September 1999
10 9 8 7 6 5 4 3 2 1

 REGISTERED TRADEMARK—MARCA REGISTRADA

Printed in the United States of America

PERCIVAL'S COUNSEL

Stranger, wandering this wood,
Come share my fire.
Share crumbs of traveler's food
And tales. Come nigher.
I know the trail you take
By mere and mire.
I've seen the cliff and lake,
With dawn afire.
Through this enchanted wood
Leads but one trail.
Richly or roughshod
Or armed in mail,
Seeking crust of bread
Or Holy Grail,
All travelers are led;
All travelers come
By this trail, home.

1

Born Knight

Knee deep in Fey forest pool, I bend to see my own, new face. Today I am new. Today I am free.

Back before dawn, I wrapped my green, "invisible" cloak around me. I took up my wee bundle of clothes, knives and fire flints, and tied my Bee Sting of poisoned darts to my belt.

In last darkness I studied the faces of my sleeping friends. (Fey eyes see in the dark like owl eyes.) I thought, *Likely, we will not meet again for a while. And when we meet, we will all be changed.*

Our branch of the Children's Guard was a small group of girls. By now the Goddess had blood-blessed all of us. It was our time to go free. We were like a nestful of fledglings trying out new wings; I was only the first to fly.

Once before, I had flown a nest. I do not now remember walking away for the last time from my mother's den. Maybe I didn't know then that it was the last time. Maybe I thought I was only going to hunt mushrooms, or play with a friend. I did not guess, then, that my first new, spirit wings were fluttering.

I do remember looking around at noon-bright trees and rocks and thinking, *I won't go back to Mama. I'll stay out here.*

Then, I suppose, I may have met one young friend, and then a new one, and then an older Guide. I must have joined the Children's Guard almost without knowing it; as a fledgeling sparrow joins a fluttering flock.

This morning my "wings" bore me away again. Light as dandelion fluff, I stepped over two girlfriends and around a third. Silent as a breeze I stole away from our clearing.

Today before dawn I grew up and ceased to be Child Guard, Child, or Guard. Today and forevermore I am simply Me: Lili of the Fey.

I bend to morning-bright water. Leaves and twigs float about my shadow. Lower I bend, searching shadow. A fresh, new face rises toward me: round, dark—big dark eyes. The mouth pouts too sweetly. Sternly I straighten my lips. Relaxed, they sweeten again.

Here under overhanging leaf-shadow my aura reflects faintly in the pool. I glimpse it as a wide, blue cloud whose edges fade in reflected sunlight.

This water-girl shows me who I am now, and who I will be for a long time to come. Later, this face will change. It will coarsen. One day it will wrinkle. But I, Lili, will still be free. Always I will be free, and always cool as this water that chills my knees and the black mud that clothes my feet. For I am Fey.

My black braid slips like a snake down my shoulder. I watch the water-girl's braid slip and drop. The two black braids reach out and touch. Shivering water, shadow and light shatter the water-girl.

Nesting blackbirds dart and call over the pool. Spring toads peep. Ahead, a twig snaps.

That will be my blundering Human friend Percy, come to meet me. Silent motion is too much to ask of Percy!

I sink cupped hands, raise cool water toward my lips.

From behind I hear a strange, faint sound: a quiet, repeated *thud*.

Cupped water halfway to thirsty mouth, I pause. Listen.

Thud! Thud!

Hah! I have heard this sound before.

I have heard it while I perched in treetops, wrapped in my green invisible cloak, watching the Kingdom outside, guarding our forest from invasion.

(Something I will never do again! From now on I will be free to live my own life and be only Me.

True it is, the Goddess will demand Her sacrifice. This debt I must yet pay. But I have time a-plenty for that.)

This repeated *thud!* coming nearer; I have heard it pass by my spy-perch many a time. Sometimes wheels creaked and squeaked, sometimes armor rattled and clanged. This is a Human Kingdom sound from the world beyond forest. Never before have I heard it in our forest! It is the sound of slow-plodding horses' hooves.

Splash! Noisy Friend Percy wades into the pool.

My eyes still look on my shadow. The water-girl is back, cupped hands halfway to sweet lips. She and I see Percy's reflection wade toward us, huge and flaming-bright, like Percy's very presence in our forest. His reflected aura ripples large and broken, orange in green water.

Always, the Children's Guard avoided Percy as a flock of blackbirds avoids an albino. Nervously, they resisted my early attempts to draw him in among us.

"You can't fish with that Percy. The fish think his hair is the sun, and dive deep."

"You can't hide with that Percy! No one could miss that blue stare of his!"

"You notice he's got hair growing on his chin?"

"He's good with darts. And that's all. What do you see in him, Lili?"

Never could I say what I saw in him. My friends were right, he was good for nothing, not even for sex play. Gods witness, he lived with his *mother*, like a toddler! I soon gave up trying to make him a Child Guard. But we met here at this pool, or in his secret tree-den, for years.

We first met on Apple Island, home of Nimway, revered Lady of the Lake. I poled a coracle over there to learn magic, for my Guide had told Nimway I had talent. I saw auras, and fairies, as few do; and once I put a small curse on a small boy who stole my string of fish. The curse worked. I don't think that boy has caught a fish yet.

There on Apple Island little Percy and little I first met, under the interested gaze of the Lady, and the anxious gaze of his big Human mother, Alanna.

The Lady's grey friend Merlin also watched us meet. Later, he watched us play. Half-Human himself, Merlin saw no harm in our romping, Fey and Human together. When we tired he brought out his harp, Enchanter, and sang us Fey songs. If I were alone, magic lesson ended, Merlin might sing me Human ballads. What very little I know of the Human Kingdom I learned from those ballads.

But Percy heard only the Fey songs, never the ballads. For his mother Alanna had begged Merlin never ever to sing to him of the Kingdom; and kind Merlin never did so.

From those ballads I learned of the Human Heart. Merlin called it the World's Greatest Magical Power.

Once he said to me, "Your friend Percy will grow a Human Heart. He doesn't know it, but it's growing now inside him."

"What about me? Don't I grow a Heart?"

"No. You are not Human, Lili. You are Fey. Be glad that Heart is not a gift of the Fey! For Heart is dangerous."

"Far as I can see, all magic is dangerous!"

Strumming Enchanter, grey Merlin nodded.

I leaned on his knee. "Mage Merlin? What Fey gift will come to me?"

"Simplicity." Merlin struck a sudden, bright chord. "Clarity." A deeper chord. "Freedom."

This last chord brought unchildish tears up in my throat.

Merlin said, "Humans rarely find any of these gifts, because of the constant clamor and uproar of their Hearts."

Still and all, I longed for a Heart!

I still do. If Heart is truly the World's Greatest Magical Power, Gods witness! I want one! (This may be what I see in Friend Percy. Maybe I hope to catch his Human Heart from him, as once I caught a cough. Maybe that's why I trouble with him at all.)

Here he comes now, *splash-splash.*

Thud! Thud! From the trail behind, three horses approach.

I lower cupped hands. Water spills back to shatter the water-girl again. I glance around.

Three dark Fey maidens flit by on the poolside trail, nearly invisible in shadow. Only the gleam of merry eyes and filed teeth betrays them. For the rest they are shadows, gowned and leaf-crowned as for a Flowering Moon dance. They vanish around the next bend. I doubt that Percy notices them.

The three coming horses carry Human riders. Alert now, I hear the rub of leather, the thump of hilt on thigh. A wave of Human odor drifts over the pool like smoke. Pffa! Never before have I smelled it so close!

Somewhere ahead, these three maidens will way-lay the three riders. First they will seduce, then kill them. No fear that these riders might leave our forest alive. How they ever entered it puzzles me. The Children's Guard should have sprinkled them with poisoned darts at the forest's edge. Unless . . . maybe the Children's Guard let them through to entertain the maidens?

I swing braid back, glance over shoulder.

Around the trail bend appears a gigantic, enormous whiteness. Big white head dips and nods. Big feet plod. An innocent, grass-eater's smell lightens the gross Human stink.

It is a great, white horse, laden with Human baggage, and with the Human giant rider himself.

Behind it appears a brown horse with another giant rider. Then a grey horse with rider. Where sunshine strikes through leaves the mixed auras of men and horses gleam orange, brown and a trace of black.

Having spied on the Kingdom often and often, I know what these riders are. They look like sun-shining Gods, clad in shirts of stone. But under the stone, they are merely giants. Human men. They are fierce and strong. They carry sharp weapons. But they are also slow, easily outwitted, easily outflitted. We Guards used to tease their kind from our treetops, laugh at them, send Fey songs downbreeze to them. They never even looked up. Slow! (Like Percy.)

I glance at Percy.

Beside me now, he stares goggle-eyed at these apparitions.

Percy never perched with the Guard in border trees. He seldom reached the forest edge at all. His mother Alanna warned him off from it. She feared that we Guards might bee-sting him. For Percy is Human, after all; and no Human who sets foot in our forest ever again sets foot out of it.

So Percy has never seen such proud and shining figures before. Come to think, Percy has never seen a horse before!

Once at this pool I saw a bright Spirit sweep great rainbow wings about itself, so brilliant as to shadow the sunrise. So now Percy's orange aura flares high above him and flames red. It sweeps itself down around Percy, and around his reflection.

Thigh deep in cold pool water, Percy stared at the advancing Gods.

Never had he seen such shining, magnificent beings. Horses he had heard of, but he had not imagined them so big, so gleaming! And never in Merlin's songs, or in his own mysterious dreams, had he a hint of such riders!

Leaf-filtered light glanced off their heads, their broad breasts. Glinting beaked caps shadowed their faces, doubtless to shield mortals from the glorious glare.

Must worship them!

They might bless him. Somehow, they might lift him up safe above his meaty, sweaty, lonely self. Or they might kill him with a glance. Gods are unpredictable.

Don't care! Now I've seen them, I can die!

Unknown, unguessed joy swept over Percy's soul like a sunrise cloud. He whispered, "Lili! Come worship these Gods with me!"

Silence from Lili.

He stole a quick sidelong glance from the Gods for Lili.

She was gone. Vanished without a ripple. The Fey had a disconcerting way of doing that.

Ho-so! If Lili feared the Gods' death-dealing glance, she did not deserve it!

Percy splashed and scrambled to leave the pool. Eyes on the Gods, he tripped on a drowned branch, fell full length, crawled out and stood up, flotsam dripping in his eyes. Wildly brushing weeds and leaves from his face, he found the trail; panting, he faced the Gods.

They had stopped dead, watching him; the first one pulled a great long, heavy knife rasping from its ornate sheath.

Percy knew what to do. After all, he worshiped God and Holy Mary every night with his mother Alanna. He crashed to his knees on the narrow trail, pressed palms together and fixed the first God with his prayerful gaze.

The God's great white horse snorted and half shied.

The rider leaned forward and looked down on Percy. Now might come the death-glance from his immortal eyes.

Percy cared not a twig. Joy like that of Alanna's angels and saints in Heaven burned away all thought of fear.

The first God raised a gloved hand, pushed back his shining cap. Pushed the long knife, rasping, back into its sheath. Laughed. His laughter rang from tree to tree around the pool.

He shouted words at Percy, to Percy. He spoke differently from the Fey. In an astounded moment, Percy understood him. *Holy Michael! He speaks Alanna talk! Human talk!*

"Ho, boy!" he shouted. "What do you there? If you love us so much, get up and lead us to shelter. Goddamn, we've got a wounded man here."

What? Shelter? Gods want shelter?

Percy's head swam with shelters to which he could not lead these Gods. Powerful as they were, he doubted they could pass the statue of Holy Mary that guarded Alanna's den. Even if they could pass, they could not squeeze their shining, giant selves into Alanna's den. Percy's own secret oak den would crash to earth under their weight. Only the Lady of the Lake's wonderful, Human-built den on Apple Island might suit them. That had stone walls and a roof, the only such in the forest! But the Lady of the Lake welcomed few guests. She would likely turn these Gods into frogs and roast them for dinner.

What did he say, wounded man! How can a God be a wounded man?

Astounded Percy found stammering voice. "Then . . . are you . . . men?"

"Are we men? Are we famished men? Ho ho! What think you, boy?"

"I took you for Gods." Percy lowered still-clasped hands.

"Gods!" The leader laughed softer this time.

"Have you never seen knights before in your dark woods?"

"I have not . . . Sir." Alanna's Human friend Old Edik liked very much to be called Sir. It always raised a smile with him, or at least erased a frown.

It had a like effect on this leader. His stern gaze softened very slightly. He pushed back his cap, revealing a grey, lined face completely framed in grey hair. *Holy Michael, he has a beard! Like me! Only thicker.*

"Hah. Huh." The knight swiveled in his saddle and said to the two behind, "Good place to camp . . . Shade . . . Water . . . This boy can bring us meat." He turned back to Perry. "You can find us meat, can't you, boy?"

"Indeed, Sir, I can!" This moment, two hares of Percy's hunting twirled over Alanna's drying fire.

Percy stood up. A good thing, because the lead knight swung heavily down from his horse to stand where Percy had knelt. Close to, Percy saw how the long knife by his side weighed him down, his stone jacket weighed him down, and blood oozed from under it.

"Sir, you are hurt!" Gods do not bleed. Truly, these "knights" were what they said—famished men.

"Goddamn! A knight of the Round Table does not call this a hurt, boy!"

"What is a knight of the rountable?"

Heavy as the leader, the second knight now dismounted and drew his knife screeching from its sheath. "God's teeth! Quit this crazy chatter!"

The leader turned back, held out a restraining hand. "No need to scare—"

"He means to hold us here, chitter-chatter, till the Enemy comes."

"No, no! The girl warned us this forest was Fey. And now we see that it is, indeed."

"This knave's no Fey!"

To Percy the leader said, "Make haste. Bring us meat, and Sir Suspicion here will let you live."

At last, caution dawned in Percy's mind. *Lo, these are in fact short-tempered, Human men. Their knives are longer than mine. They are three to my one. Curse Lili for disappearing! How by St. Hubert have they got into the forest? Where was the cursed Children's Guard? They should have repelled or killed them!*

If only I could vanish from here in a breath, like the Fey!

But soft! Consider. On the other hand . . . These are but men. I am a man. Sir Edik tells me my new beard the Fey laugh at heralds Human manhood.

Therefore, if these can shine like Gods, ride giant horses, draw huge knives, so can I! If they will tell me how.

"I will bring meat, Sir. Give me but time."

With a clang, the third, silent knight of the rountable slid down his horse and fell flat, beak-shielded nose to earth.

Three ladies spun and carded wool in Nimway's sunny courtyard.

Around them strong young greens lanced up to light between flagstones. Ancient rooms, once bright with paint and plaster, quietly decayed. Silently,

Lady Villa groaned under its ever-growing weight of vines.

Outside, the apple trees of Avalon bloomed pink and white; gathered like courtiers around their king, the mighty Counsel Oak, which crowned Apple Island.

Around Apple Island the Fey lake rippled away to far, forested shores. Well out from the magic island a few small fishing coracles drifted, dragging nets; and one coracle set off from the western shore, poled vigorously straight for Apple Island.

But the three ladies working in the courtyard did not sense its coming. Not even Nimway, Witch-Lady of the Lake, noticed its approach.

Small and dark, she perched on the rim of the long-dead fountain. White braid swung down her back into the fountain. Green gown folded quietly down over little feet. She spun carefully, watching the whorl like a Human child just learning; for indeed, Nimway was learning a Human skill her folk had never used. Unless one could see the huge white aura that misted around her, the fearsome Lady of the Lake appeared mild enough.

Human Alanna could not see the aura. But by another sense (which she called her "shivers,") she had suspected the Lady's Powers from the first. She balanced solidly on the fountain rim at a respectful distance, twirling her spindle with the absentminded skill of long, long use. Her grey braid was coiled into a crown. Her gown had once been blue. During her forest years it had faded, and been patched so many times in other faded colors that now she appeared clothed in light and shadow, fine forest camouflage.

Cross-legged on the ground at a small distance, "young" Ivie carded wool. Ivie was not Alanna's daughter, but she had always been treated as such. Of the three, she alone wore the usual Fey outfit of dun shirt and pants stolen from peasants beyond the forest. But her bright red hair, cascading wildly down into her pregnant lap, betrayed her Humanity.

Alanna glanced down at Ivie appreciatively. Maturity had clothed Ivie in beauty unguessed when she first came with Alanna to the Fey forest. *Does she regret that, now? Does she sometimes wonder what her life might have been, back in Arthur's Kingdom? Ah, well. Too late to wonder, now.*

Alanna looked around the courtyard, delighting in the spring sunshine, noticing the ruin and decay that sunshine softened. *Strange to think that Humans lived here, once! I'll wager Roman ladies sat right here in this courtyard, spinning, like us! What did the Lady say?*

"Niviene gone back to Arthur's Kingdom with Merlin."

Ah. Time to say this once again. "They go to safeguard Arthur's Peace, Lady. A very urgent mission."

"Maybe. For Humans."

"For your Fey, as well. Without the Peace their magic guards, Human enemies might come and ravage your forest."

"M-hm."

To herself, Alanna thought, *That may well happen, magic or no magic, Arthur or no Arthur.* Aloud, she said, as she had said before, "I know you miss your daughter. Well I know that pain! Yet you are blessed to have a grown daughter, Lady! You must be the only Fey in the forest to know that joy."

The Lady sighed. Her twirling spindle slowed, and idled. "My little ones grow up here, Alanna. In this villa." In courtesy to her Human friends, Nimway spoke Human words, not fluently.

"You have told us."

Predictably, Nimway continued. "Was like Human home. Safe. Solid. Like Goddess make villa, lake, island, all same time. Little ones grow. Go free in forest.

"But then come back! And back and back! And I . . . always glad to see them. Now I think . . ." Nimway fell silent.

Always before she had stopped at this point in the story. Alanna spun on, content with this. But Ivie raised serious blue eyes from her wool. This time she said, "Tell us, Lady. What do you think?"

The Lady put down her spindle. She raised her hands to finger-speak. Alanna leaned forward frowning, concentrating on the Lady's fingers.

But then Nimway seemed to remember that her Human friends barely understood finger-talk. Her hands sank again to her lap.

"I think . . . I wish . . . I let my little ones go free in forest and forget them. Like others do. Old Ways wise, after all."

"But why, Lady!" Ivie studied the Lady's face the way, as a child in the Human world, she used to study numbers drawn on slate.

"Niviene goes away, I hurt. Here." Thin fingers sketched the Lady's ribs. "Breath hard. Sun dark. Is like a . . ." The lady finger-spoke a word the Fey avoided. . . . *Sickness.*

Alanna nodded sympathy. "But then Niviene comes back. Always, she comes back."

"And I breathe again. Sun shines. But is ill, Alanna, is very ill, to see sunlight only in another's face."

"Humans call that Love."

"Love ill thing! Long I know that. My folk know it forever. Only I dare love. Pay dear! My son Lugh, he go out into Kingdom. Never come back."

"We say, 'Never is a long word.' "

"True! And no sooner do I learn that, Merlin take Niviene away with him. And I must learn again! True, now I wish I follow Fey wisdom!"

Alanna's very real sympathy mingled easily with flattery. "You are known to be wisest of all."

"Except in this. Now am old, can say, 'Aye. Took wrong step. Sacrificed to Goddess. Gave Her little ones. She lives in them now. Good.'

"But then, failed! Did not turn them free. Did not live for self. Since stole my Lugh, never live for self!"

Alanna's spindle slowed. "You stole Lugh?" From the peasants out there? "Lugh is Human?"

"Why you think he go out there? It call his blood."

"Ah . . . Men love adventure."

"Not Fey men. Lugh go back to his kind. When I little, free in forest, I tame lonesome fawn. Then, he bound away to first herd he see. Should learn lesson then!"

Ivie's carding comb lay idle on her knee. She asked, "But why did you steal the child?"

"Why? Same like others. I think I barren. Yet must sacrifice to Goddess. Half sacrifice better none."

Alanna glanced down at Ivie's grey wool. The Children's Guard stole this wool on their night raids to peasant villages. In return, the Lady gave them a share of the spun and woven cloth. Mostly, the children stole bread and cheese from the villages, but sometimes clothing; and, on occasion, newborn infants.

Softly she asked, "Lady, did you yourself go forth on a night and steal your son from a peasant hut? Or did a Child Guard bring him to you here?"

"Neither one nor other. Why ask?"

"I think . . . I seek to know you. I do not think I see you creeping into a peasant hut . . ."

"No one knows other, Alanna. Even I. See minds. Know thoughts. Not know all."

Despite years of friendship, the Lady herself knew very little of Alanna's Human life. What she knew sounded to her like a fairy story, full of dark enchantment and mystery. Long since, Alanna had given up trying to answer her constant, amazed, "*What? But why?*"

The Lady said now, "Lugh, gift."

"Gift?"

Ivie folded her hands over her unborn child. The spindle slept in Alanna's lap.

With hesitating words and finger-talk, the Lady told.

Long ago, a very young Human girl stole by night to the forest edge.

Still as a sapling in deep shadow, Nimway watched the child waver toward the forbidden tree line. Dressed in rags, hunched and stumbling, she clutched a bundle to her small chest. "I wonder. She too young to bear babe."

High in an oak a Child Guard also watched the girl, poisoned Bee Sting doubtless ready in his hand. Nimway called up to him like a bird startled out of sleep. Not even her Fey eyes could actually see this guard, wrapped in his "invisible" cloak and darkness, among a thousand leaves; but she stretched Spirit, and felt his ready hand relax. With her, he would wait and watch.

The little girl came close to the first trees, and paused. Nimway watched her peer about, up at the near-full moon and ahead, into shadowed forest. Fey eyes might have distinguished Nimway from a sapling. These keen young Human eyes passed over her without a glance.

This far a Human might come, and yet walk away.

The girl heisted the bundle higher and drew a deep breath. (Sapling Nimway in the shadows heard that breath drawn and sighed out.) She squared small, thin shoulders and walked *into the forest.*

No bird called. No poisoned dart flew.

Tall as Nimway, but too young for her burden, the girl knelt among the raised roots of the guard's oak. She laid the bundle down and made to draw back away. But the bundle cried out.

A newborn voice called out to the child mother, and to "barren" sapling Nimway.

(Later, Nimway found she had raised her arms toward that cry. Eyes on the bundle, the girl never noticed movement nearby. But Nimway had to hold her arms up and out like sapling branches till she feared they might break off.)

The child dared an angry whisper. "Shush yourself!"

The bundle cried louder. (Its cry echoed in Nimway's breasts and blood and bones.)

The girl lifted a small, thrashing figure from the bundle and bared her little breast.

Nimway and the guard above heard every eager gulp and swallow, as the infant nursed. Later, the child bent her dark head close to his and whispered. Likely she explained to him what she was doing, and why; but sapling Nimway heard no words.

He quieted. Very carefully, the child laid him down in his rag bundle between oak roots. Very carefully she leaned away back and stood up. She cast a frightened glance into the silent forest before her. Then, to Nimway's astonishment, she spoke aloud.

"You Good Folk! You allus want babes. So folks say. You come get this babe. You can have him free. You come pick him up. I can't."

As she backed away from the oak roots, a twig snapped under her heel.

She jumped like a shot hare, turned and stole quickly away out to the open field. After that one sharp sound, she likely thought she made no more.

A sleepy bird chirped behind her retreating back.

Out in the moonlit field she made an easy target.

But like a wounded hare she loped away. No poisoned dart whistled after her.

Within the forest fringe this child had seen nothing she could betray to her world. If a sapling had raised sudden branches, she had not noticed. If birdcalls had broken night silence, they meant nothing to her. She could be let go.

Ivie murmured, "She must be the only Human who ever escaped you!"

The lady shot her a baleful glance so quick a blinking eye would have missed it, and jabbed a finger signal. *So far, you* have *escaped me!*

Nimway glided forward and plucked the babe out of his rags. He lay large in her arms as in his young mother's; heavy with health, warm with sleep, buxom. "Skin soft like flower petals . . . But you know that, Alanna."

Astounded, Alanna watched a tear steal down the Lady's cheek. She had not thought the Fey could weep.

Ivie's blue eyes filled in sympathy.

The Lady blinked. She picked up her spindle and resumed work.

"Then," Alanna ventured, "you did not steal your Lugh at all. He was a gift. The mother said, 'Come pick him up.' "

"Hah! That guard think I steal him! Had his mouse spy eye on that babe, be sure!" To barter with some barren Fey.

Alanna thought aloud. "But you were not barren, Lady . . ."

"I learn that later, with Niviene. Do you two forget

what we do here?" Now the Lady spun furiously. Alanna and Ivie took up their work.

Ivie mumbled thoughtfully, "I don't think I will ever turn my child loose, free in the forest." The child in her belly thumped a visible, happy response.

"What you do, then? Keep it by you, like Alanna keep her son?"

"Why not, indeed?"

The Lady hiccuped a wee, malicious laugh. "You ever see young fellow miserable like Percy?"

Alanna gasped.

"You know this, Friend. We talk this before."

Tears dimmed Alanna's sight. Wool and spindle and her own lap swam together. "You . . . you have said this."

"More than once. Quick you forget!"

"I am only Human."

"I forget that, for love. Here we see love—confusion! What else I tell you more than once?"

"You have said . . . you say . . . my Percy . . ."

"Will leave you. Surely will, Alanna."

"No. No."

"Is only matter of time, chance. Like my lonesome fawn, Percy run to first Human herd he see."

"Ah, but he will see none! I have sacrificed my life, more life than I thought I would have, to assure that he will see none."

The Lady said quietly, implacably, "Is no assure, Alanna. Is never assure. So love is needless burden."

Alanna wiped a patched sleeve across her eyes,

looked up at the Lady. Firmly, she said, "Love is the meaning of life."

"Ha! Not even Humans think so! Ivie? You think so?"

A small voice said, "Lady!"

Startled, Alanna jumped. Her spindle rolled and fell.

At her knee stood a small person wrapped in a Child Guard's "invisible" cloak. Tearily, she watched the cloak drop away. Percy's little friend Lili drooped there, dark eyes wide, braid full of twigs and leaves. Lili panted and sweated. She must have run fast. She must have poled a coracle very fast across the lake for her small breasts to heave so under her shirt.

Calmly, the Lady acknowledged her. "Lili."

Alanna bent to pick up her spindle.

Lili gasped, "Percy . . . talking Human . . . with three Humans."

Alanna's fingers froze on her spindle.

"Humans? In the forest?" The Lady's soft voice held wonder, and threat.

"They . . . won't get out . . . But Lady, I know a little Human talk. Percy taught me."

"So?"

"Can you cast a spell so far? To stop them telling Percy about . . . Knights . . . and King Arthur . . . and the rountable?"

Darkness flooded Alanna.

She heard Ivie's frightened voice call, "Alanna!" And nothing more.

Three days I hunted Percy. Followed his scent. Rain washed it away. Followed his tracks. Lost them in a stream. Climbed to his tree-den. From the bottom of the oak I knew Percy was not there. No smell of Percy. But still I climbed to make sure there was no Percy. I tried out pool, where he had met those fool, doomed knights. No Percy.

Here and there I met Fey. "Have you seen Big White Percy?" No one had noticed him. All too busy dividing up the knights' baggage.

I even asked the fairies I saw, bright small ones and misty tall ones. They paused, as if they heard me. They looked at me, and vanished. As always.

Here it is bright evening on the third day; and I think of the Cliffs.

Why not sooner? Why not first thing?

Because the Cliffs are not part of my forest. Like everyone else I skirt around them, avoid the sight of them. The Cliffs that lean over rocky North River smell of Death.

Women who bear malformed babes usually drown them. But sometimes they toss them off the Cliffs.

Old Fey who decide to die toss themselves off. Bones wreathe the rocks of North River.

Naturally, Fey avoid the Cliffs. But not Percy. Long ago I found out that he cannot smell Death, or much else. The Lady says that's a Human trait.

Percy used to go off and play by himself at the Cliffs, when the Child Guard scoffed at him. He told me once he had rigged a vine to climb up and down.

I come to the top of the Cliffs. I hold my breath against the stink and look down over.

It's not so far down. Just far enough to kill.

Down there roaring North River boils about its rocks. Here and there, bones. Percy? I strain my eyes, searching.

No Percy.

I sigh relief, and draw back from the edge.

I smell Percy. Follow Percy smell around a boulder. There sits Percy on the edge, back to me, feet dangling over.

For a while I stand quiet, watching Percy's sturdy back. His solid shoulders. Sunset bright in his bright hair. Gods! This is my real, Big White Percy, breathing and alive; and I can hardly believe the way my ribs expand, how deep I can breathe, now I see him safe!

But soft; don't startle. Percy smells of agitation. I cannot see his aura in this clear light, but I know it must be flaming like a forest a-fire. Surprise him, he could go right over the edge.

I scratch the boulder beside me. Over and over I scratch, as if to file down my nails. Not surprisingly, Percy hears nothing at first. His ears are full of river-roar.

Louder I scratch; by now, Fey ears would notice something. Finally, even Percy notices a discordance in the river-roar, and looks over his shoulder.

"Don't watch me like that!" He roars louder than North River. "Let me know if you're watching me! Goddamn spy!"

I kneel just behind his shoulder, not right at the edge. I do not dangle my feet over. I shout, "Percy. I've been hunting you."

"For what?"

"Those Humans you talked with." We're yelling. From a distance, our words can be heard and distinguished from the river's words. I poke Percy in the back till he turns around to me. I raise my hands and finger-talk, extra slow.

They made you unhappy.

Percy shouts, "Unhappy! They opened my eyes! Now at last I see the sun!" He flings a wild hand out toward the sunset. Close to him, I feel his aura that I cannot see. It boils like North River.

I draw calm Spirit around me, a mist that Percy's heat cannot scorch. This I learned from the Lady.

Percy turns sideways, one leg dangling, and shouts in my ear. Instant talk floods out of him. He cares not that somewhere, someone may hear him. Already, we Fey are less real to him than the fantasies the knights taught him. His eager words reel and stumble and trip each other up.

I flash fingers at him. *Finger-talk, Friend!*

He tries; but his slow fingers shake and tangle, and he returns to wild yelling.

He yells about those three dead knights. He jabbers what they told him of their world. (I could have told him some of this, myself. Merlin could have sung it to him. A good thing we did not! With Percy, this knowledge acts like a . . . sickness.)

"Together, Lili! They ride together, alive or dead!"

I finger-talk. *They ride dead?*

"Listen! The High King sends them here, there, to guard the Kingdom. They ride. Fight. Together.

Anything they win they keep, so they get . . . rich. They get more and more."

More and more what?

"At home in Arthur's Dun they have a den, a . . . house, each one his own. And a . . . wife. Woman. Each one, all his own. And . . . servants, to do whatever he orders. Each one his own. But listen, this is the important part.

"They owe . . . they owe . . . allegiance to the High King. Arthur. What he says, they do. Whatever."

Like the servants. You're saying they're his servants.

"They'll die for him."

They already have.

"What do you think of that, Lili?"

Not much at all.

"Did you ever dream of such glory?"

Glory?

"Gods, Lili! Holy Archangel Michael! Knights don't live to grub a root here, a piglet there, a bit of goddamn sex!" Violently, Percy points down at the water below, now shadowed. "Goddamn *fishes* live like that! Knights live for their King, his Kingdom, their Honor! Fame! Riches! Each one his own!"

Fame? Very dangerous. Hidden is better. Fishes know that.

"You don't see! I thought you, at least, would see!"

See what?

Percy chokes.

I look up from the water to his face.

Tears spill from Percy's wide, grey eyes. Big, transparent tears like heavy raindrops wander down his cheeks into his funny yellow beard.

I stare, amazed and shocked. Attacked as by high wind, my Spirit cloak shivers around me.

"I know the others can't see it. They'd laugh. They'd say, 'Where's the glory in this . . . allegiance, hah? Where's the glory in dying for the King?' "

And where in the world is it?

"They'd say, 'Why live for somebody else? I'm plenty to live for, me myself.' "

Indeed!

"But I'm not, Lili! I'm not enough to live for! To eat and drink and fuck and shit!"

Every instinct tells me, *Get up! Run. You can't deal with this.*

I shout, "And to look at the sky."

"What? Look at the sky? The sky doesn't look back at me! I need for the sky to look back at me, Lili! I never knew that till now. That's what I need. That's why I've never been . . . happy, like all you. Goddamn, goddamn!"

Percy sobs. Softly. But the sobs shake his big, lovely form.

Instinct says, *Run!*

I hitch close up to Percy and draw my arm about his shoulder. His sobs shake me, too.

Before I climbed up here I felt watched. No living creature watched me, nothing I could hear, see or smell. Nothing that would move, roll a stone, whisper a leaf.

I feel watched now. Change watches me. The Future moves in close and watches, more invisible than Spirit. The Future stretches strange hands to grab me.

I shout into Percy's ear, "Friend, it's all right. You can do it."

"Huh?" Percy stifles a sob to listen.

"You can be a knight."

"Me?"

"Why not? You are Human. Put on a stone shirt, and you're a knight."

"Holy Michael! It's not that easy."

"And why not?"

"They told me about that, too. There's all sorts of . . . trials and . . . learnings . . . the King has to decide to knight you. Make you a knight. You don't just decide that yourself."

Very likely. Humans make everything hard and complicated.

"How can the King knight a man he never saw?"

Percy's tears quit flowing. (I breathe easier.) He dries face with fists.

"You must go out there, Friend. Meet this King. When he knows you, he will knight you."

"Go out there . . . Where? Where do I find the King?"

A pretty little shrug. But my mind whirls. "You ask as you go. 'Where rests King Arthur?' All Humans will know that. Point the way. If you mind living like a fish, if you want to live for the King, you must go find him."

Percy shouts thoughtfully, "A gigantic Adventure . . . Such as Sir Friendly described . . . Find the King, and I'll deserve knighthood!"

Finger talk. *I would think so.*

"First thing, how do I get out of the forest at all? Old Sir Edik has always told us we can never leave. He got us in. But we can never get out."

No more you can. But I can.

"Aye, well. You can go in and out at will, steal from the villagers . . . How's that help me any at all?"

I take you with me. Right now I see how.

And this is somehow true. Right now the plan rises in my mind like Apple Island out of lake-mist.

I yell, "Percy! I'll go with you!"

"You?" Percy shines at me like the sun itself. "Goddamn!" Then, ". . . But I don't know. From what those knights said, you might be more trouble than worth."

"You can use a bit of magic, Percy."

"Goddamn truth!"

"You won't make a start without me. Can't get beyond West Edge by yourself. And out there, I can sneak around, spy, vanish. You can't do that so well."

"Holy Hubert, we'll go together! Goddamn!"

I laugh in Percy's suddenly bright face. I'm not sure what this knight-word "goddamn" means, but I think I will hear a lot of it from now on.

Behind us, the Future rubs gleeful hands together.

In his excitement Percy has not asked me why I want to go. So much the better.

With the Lady of the Lake, I walk among flowering apple trees.

We glide from tree to trunk, from shadow to

shade, through ringing, insistent birdsong. I draw my "invisible" cloak about me. The Lady's green gown melts into green shadow. No one looking up from the lake would notice color, or motion. No one closer would hear our words; for we use finger-talk, and gentle murmurs which even we can hardly hear over the birdsong. Invisible, inaudible, we move among the blooms of Apple Island like two drifting spirits.

Nimway says, "This is a quest you speak of. A long, dangerous adventure in search of treasure, such as Merlin sings."

I sign, *Percy quests for Knighthood. I quest for a Human Heart.*

And why?

For Power, Lady! Merlin says the Human Heart is the World's Greatest Power.

"Look at me, Lili. Have you seen greater Power?"

Mid-step, I pause; look carefully. Nimway casts on me her sharp, dark glance that sees through matter to mind and spirit. In dappled shade her huge white aura shimmers softly.

I shake my head. I have never seen more Power in a living being.

"But I have no Human Heart. Nor have I ever gone questing."

I must do this.

We move on.

Nimway murmurs, "If I consent, your Percy will be the first Human ever to leave this forest."

I remind her, "Merlin."

"Merlin is half-Fey."

"Percy grew up here, Lady."

"Unwilling!"

"He has given his word, he will keep the Forest secret forever."

Nimway grins briefly. "His word!"

"His word is sacred. Alanna taught him that. And then those knights, they told him the same. Percy will keep his word."

Nimway says, "Strangely, I agree."

Relief! The Lady will not stand in our way!

She says, "I know Alanna."

"Yes."

"Her son will keep his word. I also know something from Merlin and Niviene about the Kingdom out there. Lili, will you listen to counsel?"

Very gladly.

Drifting, gliding slowly uphill, the Lady advises me.

"Pretend you live in a Merlin ballad. If the song ends, so do you. In this ballad, you are a spy in unknown country. No one may guess who or what you are."

I understand.

"Firstly, then, never open your mouth."

???

"Eat carefully. Smile and laugh, close-mouthed. Humans notice filed teeth."

!!!

"Second. You cannot be invisible out there. You cannot take cover, for there is none. But you can be unnoticed."

"Next to Percy?"

Together we laugh, openmouthed, silent.

"Easiest next to Percy! For all eyes will be on him. Thirdly, then, remain chaste."

???

"You are virgin, now."

How can she be so sure? Ah. My aura tells her. Dark eyes unfocused, she gazes past me into Spirit. She says, "Stay virgin. Sex steals Power. The strongest mages are chaste."

Chaste? Once more I pause, mid-step.

What of the Goddess? What of Her sacrifice?

"Time enough ahead."

But Nimway is far from chaste! She lives with Merlin. She poles across the lake to every Flowering Moon dance. Mischievous at her age, she still waylays handsome Human men on twilit forest fringes, seduces and kills them.

But you, Lady?

She smiles, close-mouthed. "I choose not to use that method. Merlin tells me that if I did, I would be twice as strong."

Then why? . . .

Hold yourself chaste. Fourthly . . . We walk on. "Humans are proud."

"Like Percy."

"Heed their manners, their courtesies. Do nothing at all until you see how others do. Sit when they sit, bow when they bow, call them Sir. You speak the language?"

"Some. Percy and Merlin have taught me. Percy will show me the courtesies, too."

"Percy, hah! You must teach Percy."

We pause at the edge of a sunny glade. Across this golden space rises the great Counsel Oak, King Tree of Apple Island. He casts a shadow like night.

Nimway says. "We will ask Oak-counsel."

Have I not just received counsel?

But wait.

Her chin points downwind.

Undergrowth rustles.

Whiteness pushes gently out of a thicket.

I am reminded of the white horse Percy's first knight rode; but this whiteness is small, and careful.

Head and shoulders lift into sunlight; leafy ears flick. This is a small fallow doe.

Spirit-white, she steps out halfway into golden light. Wobbling nose smells us. Golden eyes blink at us. She looks away, waits a moment more, leaves her thicket altogether and minces across the open space, twitching her tail at every step. Counsel Oak's deep shadow swallows her up.

Nimway finger-speaks. *Our guide leads the way.*

But we wait a moment ourselves, looking, listening, testing air, before we dart across the space swift as swallows, into oak-night.

Here it is too dim for finger-talk. Birdsong above is lost in a constant, windy rustle of high leaves. The scent of magic drowns all scent of bark, bud, moss or mouse.

Close to the trunk and its great black lightning-

cave, Nimway asks me, "You truly will go on this
quest?"

"I will."

"Had I known you would leave us, I would have
taught you more, and faster."

I think myself well taught! I see the invisible. My
spells work.

"I wish you had learned to make fire . . . Niviene
tells me that Power is most valuable, out there."

True, I have not yet learned that. Not for lack of trying!

"I cannot teach you quickly what needs years to
learn. But, I have a gift for you."

Nimway lays fingertips to the thong about her neck.
From under her gown she draws up a dangling charm.
Lightly held in fingertips it looks like not much, grey,
metallic. The scent of Power flows from it.

Desire like lust floods me.

Nimway says, "Merlin gave me this ring." She
holds it with fingertips apart, so I can see it clearly
in the dim light.

"Victory in her name. This is her song." Softly,
she chants.

> *"Sword for fight,*
> *Feathers for flight.*
> *Hound on trail,*
> *Wind in sail.*

Sing her those lines if you feel her Power ebb. Thus
you strengthen her, and she will strengthen you, in
every way."

My hand reaches by itself, drawn to Victory.

The Lady steps back away. "Yet another virtue she has. Point her at another, and she will strengthen him."

The ring calls to me. My hand stretches after her. The Lady steps back away, up against Counsel Oak's rough trunk.

"She is made to fit a Human finger, and would slide off yours. Keep her around your neck . . . Lili. Out there, you may meet my son. My Lugh."

Ah, yes. The long-lost one. Give me the ring!

"Merlin and Niviene tell me he is well. They say he is famous in the Kingdom. Merlin sings me ballads about him.

"But you, Lili; you may see what they do not. When Victory brings you back here safe, come and tell me about my Lugh."

"Lady, I will try." I reach again for the ring.

"Wait." Holding the ring away, the Lady takes my reaching hand and lays it against Counsel Oak's bark.

"Feel."

Despite my urgent greed for the ring, I feel the oak's Power warm my palm.

"Listen."

The constant gentle breeze that plays in Counsel Oak's shade rustles his leaves.

"Listen."

Almost waggling my ears like the white doe, I listen. The leaves whisper.

Dread stands close behind me in Oak-darkness. Dread reaches a long finger, taps my shoulder.

Nimway's dark gaze pierces mine.

"You hear, Lili?"

"I hear."

"Enough to turn back most Fey!"

"Not this Fey."

"You must have Human blood in you!"

"Who can ever know that?" *I know not my own mother, never mind my ancestors!* "Lady, give me the ring!"

Nimway lifts the thong and its ring from her neck. Carefully, she lets it down over my head. She even pulls my braid through and over the thong, and pats it down in place; and her fingertips set Victory dangling safe, between my breasts.

"Alanna!"

For a while, a voice had been speaking through a darkness where rushes flared, infants wept, slaves rushed about, yarn tumbled and tangled.

"Alanna!"

Once more the voice spoke, loudly, firmly. Behind closed eyelids Alanna came awake.

Don't want to wake.

Filtered sunshine waited behind closed eyelids. Something else waited, too, just behind the torn curtain of sleep. Something like . . . sorrow.

Sorrow? Once I knew sorrow all too well.

"Alanna!"

She opened her eyes.

What was this rough wicker wall before her? What was this curving, messily thatched roof, not much taller than herself? Birdsong from outside replaced the cry of dream-children. Instead of frightened feet scurrying on stone floors, now she heard and recognized the voice that called her.

"Sir Edik?"

Alanna sat up.

There in the doorway he stood, holding back the deerskin curtain he had hung for her. Sunlight silvered his grey curls and beard. Where she or Ivie, or dear Percy, God knew! had to stoop a little, he stood erect.

How easily he has fit into this enchantment! He has almost turned Fey himself since we came here to . . . to . . . Holy Mary! Now I remember.

Sorrow stepped through the unraveling rags of sleep and glared at Alanna.

Desperately, she wanted to sink back, pull darkness around her and run stumbling down the long, stone stairway of her past. Away down there at the bottom, after many a turn and startle, after a thousand pains and griefs—away down there spread a sunlit garden where a small girl lay in lavender and squinted happily through leafy, flowery light.

But that small girl had been born—and would be very severely trained—to be a lady.

Alanna said softly, "Sir Edik, come in."

Like Sorrow, he entered.

Alanna sat up straight and lifted her thick grey braid back over her shoulder, all she could do to tidy herself. Sir Edik sank down cross-legged beside her pallet. His shrewd, brown eyes sought hers kindly. "You are recovered, Alanna?"

"Recovered? I will never recover." Fully awake, she looked ahead to endless, heart-squeezing misery.

Sir Edik spoke quietly. "My dear, you know it is the way of nature that Percy should leave you. In the way of the Fey he would have left you years ago. By now, you would hardly know which handsome young fellow he was—except that he stands out like a rose in a turnip field."

Proudly. "You mean, like a white buck in a dun herd."

"Say it how you will. You could not so well forget which young Fey he was. Even so—"

"We are not Fey, Sir Edik! We are Human. And in the Human way—"

"In the Human way Percy would have gone to be a page years ago. He would now be a squire, maybe a knight, fighting for King—"

"We escaped that! We came all this way to . . . to this!" Alanna swept a work-scarred hand around at the wretched, patched bower and all its wretched, mended mats and tools. "We came here to escape Kings and Chivalry! To keep Percy safe!"

"Aye. And you have kept him safe all these years. But not forever. Being Human, you cannot expect safety forever. Either way, Human or Fey, now you lose Percy." Very kindly, Sir Edik spoke cruel words.

A great groan escaped Alanna. "I am alone!" Alone for all mortal time. And now, despite all training and practice, tears dimmed her sight. The homely curved bower-wall faded, melted, and dribbled down before her eyes.

"Not so, dear. You have Ivie with you."

Mortified, Alanna wiped her eyes on her patched gown. "Hah!" *Ivie, indeed!* "Without Percy—"

"You have me."

"You, Sir Edik?"

"Gladly would I stay beside you forever, even here in this bower, though I like not to sleep two nights in the same den."

She stared into his small, brown face; his steadfast, mild gaze. "You . . ."

"You know I love you."

Well, surely you do!

Alanna had always known that. It was easier not to know it, better to forget it. But underneath, in her secret heart, she had known it since . . .

He told her. "I have loved you since Sir Ogden brought you home as his bride."

I remember. Too well I remember! (Smoky torches; stamping, blowing horses; Sir Ogden's gloved hand hard on her horse's rein; and Edik's face—small and brown as now—at her knee. He gave her a long glance before he bowed.)—*I knew it even then.*

"But . . . You dance with the Fey to the Flowering Moon."

(Flowering Moon times, Alanna closed herself and Percy in the bower, and young Ivie. But Ivie had been missing, lately. Alanna and Percy now huddled alone, listening to three threatening drums throb

from three directions, and the occasional shriek of
a pipe.

"I have seen you on your way to dance!" (Once she
had met him on a narrow trail. He was hurrying
toward the Flowering Moon drum as she hurried away
from it. She had been grieved and shocked to see him
decked out like an amorous Fey in crisp, new-stolen
shirt, and flowers flopping in his grey curls. Safe inside,
she had murmured to Percy, "I thought Sir Edik was
Christian, and our friend. But he dances to the Moon."
Sullenly, Percy had murmured, "He always did. You
didn't want to know it.")

Now, patiently, Sir Edik asked her, "Do you wish
me not to dance because you do not?"

Ah! We can quarrel a bit. Forget this other matter . . .
"By now, you must have lain with every woman in
the forest!"

"Alas, no."

Alanna blushed hot.

"But if I had, what of it? I do not love every
woman in the forest. I love you. I love you as I did
when you were Percy's age, working with your
women in Sir Ogden's castle garden. Alanna, you
were a woman, then. You bore Sir Ogden's first son
in your body. Now Percy is a man. But you will not
let him go forward into manhood."

Alanna bowed her head down, not to meet Sir
Edik's reproachful brown gaze.

"Now, in the way of nature, take me into your
bower. Let Percy go. Alanna, if the Lady of the Lake,
a heartless Fey, will let him go, surely your mother's

heart must do the same! For he must go, or the life
in him will die like an unhatched bird."

"Sir Edik, if Percy goes away from me, my heart
will break in two." Alanna folded protective hands
over it.

"My dear, you think that love breaks your heart."
Sir Edik's hand stole onto Alanna's knee. She sat
bowed, looking down at this small, brown hand. "It
is not love, but fear. You think of yourself being
alone, and fear burns your heart and ribs."

"If I did not see Percy coming to me . . ." She
imagined him bumbling toward her across her small
clearing, swinging a hare for the fire. Like her dead
husband he strode, strong and direct, caring not a
pinecone that his footfalls echoed in earth. (Not like
the maddening little Fey, flitting about like ghosts!).
His broad shoulders were thrown back. His golden
hair—Sir Ogden's hair, before it greyed—flamed sunshine. True, a cloud lay across his dear face, which
should look fresh, honest and open. Still, the imagined sight of him raised heart and head till Alanna
looked Sir Edik in the eye again.

He was saying, "Fear rules you, Alanna. Love
would bid you send Percy forth to be a man. Give
him the tools, give him the knowledge he will need
and let him go."

"But . . ." *Aha!* "I have no tools to give him."

Sir Edik's brown eyes rose slightly to the shelf he
had built over her doorway. Sir Ogden's rusted
sword lay there, pushed back and shrouded. Hidden.

Alanna almost gloated. "One sword . . . one dull

old sword he has never seen or touched, let alone learned . . . Sir Edik, your wits have taken leave of you. You would have me send my only living child away into that terrible world with nothing but an old sword . . ."

But lo! Over Sir Edik's shoulder, through a rent in the deerskin curtain, Alanna saw Percy enter the clearing. He came brighter, sturdier, happier, than she had just imagined him. The cloud of sullen misery had lifted from his face.

He had not gone yet. She still had this one chance.

With a cry she sprang up, started forward, stumbled over Sir Edik and fell into his lap.

He tried to hold her.

She struggled and flailed. She rolled away and up and out the door to Percy.

Once when we were young, Percy tried to show me that Alanna's Goddess Mary was harmless.

He said, "Stand right here." And he set me firmly before Her. "Get used to Her. You'll see She's just wood."

I knew She was wood! But I also saw the blue cloud of Her aura flame toward me, that aura Percy never saw.

He had to hold on to my hand to keep me there. That first moment I was gut-anxious. Next, my hair started to rise. Shudders scrambled up and down me. My heart began to pound like a Flowering Moon drum. I tore my hand from Percy's and ran. I did not see Percy again for many days.

A foolishly well-worn trail leads straight up from West River to Alanna's bower. As you enter the clearing you feel Mary's Power. You stop and look about, and then you see Mary.

She stands under Her own bower, which looks like a Fey-built shelter; except that it stands clear and visible and isolated as the Counsel Oak King Tree.

Mary Herself is my size, and mostly grey; though traces of blue and red color cling to Her gown. A tiny man stands upright on Her left palm. He wears a long robe and a rayed reed sunhat, such as Humans wear out haying. His face is sad and severe. Percy says that He is Mary's "Babe."

Mary's right hand stretches out toward you. Percy says it offers you protection and comfort. I feel it seeks to grab me and make me as small as Her Son. Then I could stand on Her right palm forever, a stiff warning to passing Fey.

Mary's face is grim as Alanna's. She wears a tall, pointed crown because, Percy says, She is Queen of Heaven. Her figure and hair are lost in heavy, draping robes.

If Mary's Babe is a severe man She holds on one hand, what must Mary be, Herself?

Spirit lives in Her. Her blue aura drifts about Her, undimned by sunshine. It says She is more than alive. Fey who do not see auras at all can still feel the presence of this one. Come close to Mary, and you feel someone breathing. Stand before Her and Her empty wooden eyes look at you. Step right or left, and they seem to follow you.

Seeing all this, if you are Fey, you turn back. We call the clearing "Mary's Clearing."

No one wants to pass anywhere near Mary. I have never seen fairies, ghosts or any kind of spirit near Mary but Her own blue aura. And I have spent much time, over the years, spying from this high yew on the edge of Her clearing!

Right now as I look down at Her, Mary's aura prickles and turns toward me, watches me. Even "safe" and high in my yew tree, I shiver.

Animals and Humans do not fear Mary. Right now, sparrows are building a nest in Her thatched roof. Several times a day Ivie comes by lugging wood or water; she bows her fiery head to Mary, as to anyone she might meet on a trail, and walks on by without missing a step.

Sometimes Mary wears a flower crown on top of Her wooden crown. Then I know that Ivie, or Alanna, has actually stepped up close and laid these flowers on Her. It must be they cannot even feel the pulse and throb of Her great, blue aura!

Percy has no fear of Her. And yet, I have seen him kneel before Her, raise his hands and pray—even as the Lady prays to the Goddess. At these times I sometimes see Mary shine on him, and his face and upraised hands glowing with Her light. I do not watch this. I turn away.

Blackbirds sing now around me. Insects hum and whine. From Alanna's bower I hear voices, but not what they say. They talk Human, which I don't know that well. But the tones tell me that Alanna is awake and frightened, and gentle Old Sir Edik is trying to calm her.

Why is Alanna so often frightened? Does she lack the powerful Human Heart she should have? Or maybe she does not know how to use it. A magic wand in an ignorant hand is of little use.

Crack! Snap! Thud! That's Big White Percy, coming up behind my yew.

He strides by without a glance up the yew, never dreaming my presence; no scent, no breath alerts him. If I spoke, he would hear only blackbirds singing. In shadow his aura glows wide, orange and green. He swings into the clearing. Sun burns in his hair, and his aura fades.

Inside the bower, Alanna shrieks.

Percy breaks stride with a little, small jump, like a dart-struck hare. Quickly, then, he gathers himself and advances again on the bower.

The deerskin curtain is ripped aside. Alanna charges out, arms stretched to Percy, mouth wide with a shriek.

Sir Edik, following, stops in the entrance. There he pauses, arms folded, curly grey head cocked. Shadowed, his green aura ripples around him. Like me he spies, unobserved.

Alanna hurls herself against Percy. He rocks back on his heels and flings his arms around her to hold her up. She sobs a torrent of Human words at him. "Mother . . . break . . . stay . . ."

Hah! Percy said to me that Alanna would not let him go out to the Kingdom, even if the Lady of the

Lake allowed it. I said to Percy that she could not stop him. How could she stop him? Percy growled and glared.

Now I see. These words, these cries, are weapons that wound a Human Heart. As Mage Merlin told me, Heart is dangerous.

Percy answers at first with murmurs, then with clear words. "Knight . . . King . . . Sky . . ." Alanna shudders and threatens to fall at each of these words, so Percy has to hold her up tighter. They are two trees that lean together, swaying in a high wind. I have seen some strange Human things from this yew, but nothing stranger than this.

Alanna hiccups and squawks. Leaning on Percy, she beats his shoulders, his arms, with her fists. "Listen!" she gasps, and follows with a string of incomprehensible words. "Listen!" Another string. "Listen to me. I was there, I know!" And another string. She's telling him about the Kingdom, how fearful and terrible it is.

She's telling him what he must do there—how he must walk, talk, breathe, so as to be Human. So as to survive.

Gods! I'm grateful I walked away from my mother while she slept! I'm glad I don't remember her face.

Percy murmurs understanding.

Alanna pushes herself upright and away. But she still grips Percy's hand. She points past him to Mary. She turns him around by his hand and leads him to Mary; as I have seen a peasant woman lead a bull by its nose ring.

Alanna expects Mary to help her. But why? Percy told me that Mary's son went away from Her, too.

Alanna crashes to her knees before Mary. She pulls Percy down beside her and screams.

All through this storm Mary has been quietly glowing, without even me noticing. Now I notice, because the quiet glow becomes lightning. As a lightning flash brightens river and forest, so Mary's flash brightens Her clearing. But this lightning holds its glare. Stark light stronger than sunlight illumines Percy's and Alanna's upturned faces; and Sir Edik, who thought himself safe in the doorway; and a mouse who thought himself safe in Mary's shadow.

The clearing hangs in light deeper than sunlight for as long as it takes me to skitter down my yew and flee. Longer. For even as I dart away, heart pounding, from tree to tree and shade to shade I can still glance back and see that unearthly light above Mary's clearing.

Up and down the Fey river drums beat for the Flowering Moon.

Gently we drift, Percy and I, in our bobbing round coracle, downstream toward the Kingdom. (Far enough upstream is also the Kingdom. Everywhere around our magic forest is Arthur's Kingdom.)

Percy and I have always been alone together, but never quite like this. This time we go alone together on a long trip, maybe an endless trip. So we bring our material goods with us: fire flints, Bee Stings, clothes. Alanna gave Percy her big soup kettle, to serve as a helmet; I wonder how she will cook soup, now. She's used that kettle for longer than I've known Percy! Also, she made him a new tunic in a hurry, from three different-colored cloths.

(Giggling, I asked Percy if she had made one like that for me. "Oh," he said, "maybe she would have; but I did not tell her you were going."

"Why not?"

Percy blushed from the bobbin in his throat to the roots of his hair. "You know how she is . . ."

Ah, yes. This very night, Alanna probably hides in her bower from the Flowering Moon drums.)

We drift past Apple Island, where Lady Villa gleams moon-white through its creeping, sheltering vines. We drift carefully downstream from one drum to the next, because this way is the most silent. Percy mans the pole. *Plop!* goes the pole like a jumping frog, and we skim forward. *Crrrsh!* goes pole against bank, like a turtle bumping its shell, and we waver out into moonlit water. Another *plop!* brings us back under the safer shadow of overhanging trees.

Behind us one drum fades. Around the bend, another throbs. Now we are close enough to hear pipes. Gods! We're close enough to see firelight reflected from white birches on the shore! Red light leaps, interrupted by leaping shadows.

Back in there they are dancing. All my friends, all my folk, dance tonight at this fire, or some other. Even most of the Children's Guard have left their posts on the forest edges to dance tonight. (A good thing no Humans know this! Tonight they could invade with little danger—at least at first.)

Percy and I chose this good night for our escape. Despite the Lady's consent, we decided to escape, attracting no notice. Not all the Children's Guard may have heard the Lady's decision; and any way, we Fey are not known for obedience or cooperation! So we chose this Flowering Moon dance night.

But I do not trust wholly to the Fey dance-lust. I also cast a very fine magic mist about our coracle. Any who may chance to notice it will rub their eyes and blame the moonlight.

Back in the trees, the pipe wails like Alanna. *Thump!* Goes the drum, like my heart.

Never since I was very young have I missed a dance! We children danced around the edge of the crowd. We learned the steps. We tasted the Grand Mushroom the dancers nibbled, and learned its uses. We watched the glances and gestures, the glidings away and drawings together. When the adult dancers had disappeared, two by two, sometimes three together, we slept where we dropped around the dying fires.

Last autumn for the first time, a young fellow strutted up to me. And for the first time I observed that under his beautiful costume, he himself was beautiful.

I wished he had been Percy! If only he had been Percy!

Well I knew that Percy was shut away in Alanna's bower.

Come to think, I remember that Ivie danced at that same fire. I remember her hair flopping loose, red as the fire. Big she is, heavy for Fey taste; though I supposed a Human fellow might like her. So I was surprised when she wandered off into darkness with a fine Fey man lovelier than mine.

(I doubt that Ivie dances tonight, great with child as she is.)

I wanted Percy. I looked at my beautiful fellow, and I wanted Percy! His bright bigness! His warmth!

That night I waited for Percy. Later nights, I still waited for Percy. But Percy never came to dances. Alanna kept him shut in with her during Flowering Moons.

I was young. Desire was not yet hot in me. Even so, I tried to interest Percy at other times—while fishing, reed gathering, trapping together.

Percy was never interested. Percy is never interested. My friends remark that he is made of ice. Slowly, I grow hot.

Drifting now past firelight and music, sadness seizes me.

Why am I leaving my folk and my forest?

This Human Heart I want so much, is it truly the World's Magical Power, as Merlin tells? It does Alanna little good! And Ivie . . . well, Ivie seems to lack it. Ivie has become almost Fey. And Percy has not yet grown his Heart; he doesn't know he has one.

So I have only Merlin's tales to go by; Grey-bearded half-Human Merlin told me once of this famous Human Heart and its Powers . . . and dangers.

And now for this I slide downriver with Percy on a quest I know better than to dare!

Good-bye, Flowering Moon drum!

Good-bye—the last fading drum throbs. *Good-bye.*

Ahead, the Fey river narrows. Leaning tree-shadows darken water. Percy leans on his pole, holding us still.

Rustle. Slither. Whispering *splash.*

Something leaves the dark bank and swims out into moonlight.

Whiter than moonlight, it breaks river-sparkle.

It turns an eye toward us, flaps an ear and calmly swims for the far shore.

I murmur, "Deer."

"White!"

"Our guide."

"Huh?"

"Shush."

Percy poles us forward.

Trees fall back, draw away.

This is the border, the dangerous crossing. Child Guards may yet watch here.

I concentrate, touch a fingertip to Victory who sings near my heart, and send deeper, denser mist around our coracle.

Behind us the Flowering Moon drum beats like a forgotten heart.

Before us, the Flowering Moon silvers a new, wide-opening landscape.

OAK COUNSEL

A price is paid for every Quest.
Draw heart's blood from out bared breast.
Spin soft silk of needly nettle,
Boil beef broth without a kettle.
Sort grain from grain, and pile apart.
Be still, when silence breaks the heart.
Raise the rock and seek the stair
That descends from light and air
To the dread domain of Death.
(Eyes averted. Bated breath.)
Open not the box you bear
Back up that steep stony stair;
Bring up treasure, honest measure.
Even so, your Quest may fail.
Who has found the Holy Grail?

2

Never Knight

In a ray of spring light from an arrow slit, Alanna sat nursing newborn Percy. He sucked manfully at her breast. His milky blue eyes wavered, chubby hands waved. She tucked his soft, kicking feet securely under one arm and cradled him in the other.

Percy was the ninth son whom Alanna had nursed herself. Always, the nurse brought the child to her swaddled, tight-bound to a cradleboard. Always, she undid the bands, lifted babe from board and cuddled him, soft skin to softer skin. Now again, as eight times before, Alanna's heart enfolded her newborn, body and soul.

But this time, the heart beneath the milk-rich breast was broken.

King Arthur's messenger had left her . . . judging by the slant of arrow-slit light, an hour ago.

Sir Ogden, her lord for twenty-five years, was dead; and not in battle, and by no deadly illness. Unhorsed in a festive joust, Sir Ogden had broken his neck.

This milk may give Percy colic!

This brokenhearted milk. *But*—Alanna smiled a bit grimly at the thought—*Not this babe! This one could nurse on blood!*

Percy was the biggest, strongest babe she had ever borne. He had cost her more pain and weakness than even her first; here he was a week old, and still she could hardly sit on the bench without cushions and folded cloaks beneath her.

Now, of twenty-five years' pains and loves, Percy was all she had left.

One by one, her little sons had grown into fighting men—Knights. What else could they be? Cabbage seeds grow to be cabbages, and Knights' sons, like dragon's teeth, grow to be Knights. But he that lives by the sword dies by the sword, and they all had died, not all directly by the sword, but all in the midst of knightly pursuits.

And now this sorry story will tell itself again. Another soft, sweet child will cut himself a sapling sword and duel with peasant boys till he gets his sword of steel . . .

If I could take Percy away to some far land! A land where men are content to spend their strength on field and farm, and are honored for it! But that land is farther off than I can think.

In the gathering shadows behind Alanna floor rushes rustled. Someone came softly, slowly, dragging a graceful hem.

Ivie.

Sir Ogden's ward, daughter of his murdered brother, Ivie was nearly fifteen. *For ten years now, she has been as my daughter. For God gave me none of my own. I have trained and taught, nursed and comforted like a mother. And now she learns her final fate. Now I must comfort again, biting my own grief back.*

Ivie came gently into the arrow-slit light. She dropped her small curtsy and folded competent, square hands at plump waist. Only the long, fiery red braid looped down her shoulder warned of possible fire within.

When grief-heavy Alanna did not speak, Ivie murmured, "You sent for me, Lady."

Alanna shifted Percy to her other breast and heaved a releasing sigh.

"You have heard the news."

"Of Sir Ogden. The hall below buzzes with it. My Lady, I am sorry!"

Alanna glanced up sharply. Ivie's young face, smooth with innocence, looked back calmly.

Naturally. Ivie never spent any time with Sir Ogden. To her, he was ever only a strong, always busy figure striding past. She grieves not for him, nor, yet, for herself.

"Have you thought what this means to you, yourself?"

"Ah . . . ?" *She's had little time to think.*

"Ivie, fetch a stool. Sit here by me . . . There. You are well set?"

"Aye, Lady." *Still the soft, docile voice! She has yet caught no clue, no thread to this tapestry.*

"You will not fall off the stool."

"Why, no, lady!"

"Ivie. The King's messenger told me of my Lord's

death." Ivie nodded, slow and sad. "He also told me
that this hall will now belong to Sir Ryan Ironside."

What! A glint of surprise? Maybe curiosity?

"You remember Sir Ryan?"

"Ah, yes. Somewhat." *She has seen him stride past
her with Sir Ogden, rumbling oaths and threats to unknown enemies. She has seen him dine with Sir Ogden,
fast and furious. She had to lean over his massive shoulder
to refill his goblet. Once, I remember, seven times in a
row!*

"You are to wed him."

No response.

There. Percy is satisfied. His sweet eyes close. . . .

Slowly, Ivie's smooth face froze.

"What think you, Ivie?"

Ivie licked lips, bowed head, looked up again.

"Speak."

Ivie managed it. "I? *I* wed Sir Ryan Ironside? . . .
I mean . . . why not you, Lady?"

Alanna shuddered so hard, Percy's blue eyes
drifted open.

She counseled herself, *It is but a natural thought.
Given Ivie's age, and my own . . .*

She explained. "Ogden Hall remains with Sir Ogden's blood, Ivie. I am to wed, also; wherever the
King decides." *When does a woman rest?*

"I . . . Ah . . . Oh!" Pure crystal welled in Ivie's
blue eyes and rolled down paled cheeks.

"It may not be so bad, Ivie."

"Sir . . . Sir *Ryan*! Holy blessed Mary, Queen of
Heaven!" Tears flooded down Ivie's frozen face.

"Oh, come! You always knew—"

"But, but, *him*!"

"Ivie, we have seen worse men."

"Not me! I've seen no one worse!" Hiccup.

Percy sleeps.

Rushes rustled back in the shadows. Alanna eased Percy down on her knees and drew a scarf over her breasts.

"My Lady Alanna," said a kind voice at her shoulder, "I've brought you strengthening ale."

Ivie wept on, head erect, face still frozen.

Edik stepped into the shaft of light.

Sir Ogden's trusted steward was small, dark and ageless, but for occasional grey curls among the black. Thoughtful as always, he alone in the hall had come to offer Alanna solace in this hour of grief.

Unsurprised, she thanked him with a deep nod. "Leave it here beside me, Edik. I'll drink it if I can."

Lithely he crouched, brushed rushes aside and placed the full goblet by her feet. Crouched, he laid a bold, brown hand on Ivie's knee. "You have heard your own news, I see."

Alanna bit back a comment on his forwardness. *He's been like a younger uncle to her. Now he can help comfort her.*

Ivie gurgled, "I'm to wed . . . Sir Ryan Ironside!"

Edik patted her knee, as he might pat a sick dog. "So they say down in the hall. They are pleased, Ivie. They say, at least we will still have you here."

"I wish . . . I wish . . ."

"What is your wish, child?"

Alanna breathed a feeble protest. "Edik, you reach too far!"

He turned soft brown eyes to her. "Lady, what if I could grant her wish?"

Ivie blurted, "I wish I could go somewhere! Where I could choose my own husband! Or none! None at all! If only there were such a place in the world . . ."

Pat, pat, pat. Edik turned back to Ivie. "I know just such a place."

"Wha . . . what?" Ivie gulped back grief.

What can he mean?

Pat, pat, pat. "Not very far off, neither."

Alanna's heart flopped over like a great, caught fish.

"Edik! What can you mean?"

He kept his face to Ivie. Over his shoulder he asked Alanna, "Lady, have you also a wish?"

Almost, she laughed. *What folly we talk in despair!*

"Naturally, Edik. We all have wishes."

He turned to her.

"And what is yours?"

"Why! That I could take my babe here to some far, unknown place, where he need never be Knight!"

"The same place Ivie longs for. It is not so far."

"There truly is some such place?"

"Within sight of here."

Oh, God! Can he mean what I think?

"Stand up, Lady. Stand up, Ivie. Look out the slit."

Alanna laid sleeping Percy against her shoulder. Cramped from long sitting, weighed down by grief, she rose slowly to the arrow slit. Already there, eager Ivie leaned into light.

Edik said behind them, "On the horizon."

Aye! What I thought!

Ivie whimpered. "Nothing there, Edik."

They looked down across Alanna's garden, where Holy Mary's statue stood guard under a vine-laden lattice. With the servants, they had barely commenced to spade here. They looked farther down, across Sir Ogden's three villages, farmlands, pasture lands, bare-boughed woodlots, all shining brown and gold in spring light. Beyond all, shone the distant, pale orange smudge of the forbidden, Fey forest.

"See you not the forest, yonder, young Ivie?"

Ivie dried her eyes on her sleeve and looked again. "I see only the . . . the Fey forest."

"There, you can choose your own man."

"There!"

"There, Lady Alanna, you can raise your son to be a man, and never a Knight."

Holy Mary! Help me now!

Alanna faltered. "But, Edik . . . How would we live, there?"

"You asked that not, before. You asked only for a land where Percy would not grow to be Knight. There is the land."

"Nonetheless . . ." Alanna swallowed the spit of fright. "To raise him at all, any way, I must live somehow."

"There, you will live by your own hands and wits."

Ivie murmured, "How would we enter there, Edik? I have always heard that none who entered there came out alive."

"I can take you safely in."

You can?

Alanna and Ivie turned round to face Edik. Spring light glinted in his greying, black curls, in his squinting, suddenly merry, brown eyes.

I thought I knew this man, my Lord's steward! I knew him loyal, dedicated, truthful . . . loving. What more may be there to know? What secret has he kept, all these years?

Ivie asked, "But . . . once in . . . how would we ever come out again?"

"You would not."

"Not ever?"

"Not ever. Think not to go, young Ivie, if you will ever wish to return."

Holy Mary! "Percy!" Alanna cried softly, "Percy could never return from there?"

"He could not, Lady."

"Then . . . the King's long arm could not reach him there!"

"It could not."

New, unknown strength stiffened Alanna's arms. Sleeping Percy stirred and wiggled against her grip. "But would he hear tales, songs, of Knighthood and Chivalry?" *Well I know the power of such songs!*

"Unlikely."

"So he would never know what he had missed, I mean, what he had been saved from!"

"He would think himself a Fey, Lady, like those who live there."

Fey. Good Folk. I must think again on this . . . The Good Folk have no goodness, no virtue, no Honor.

"Ah . . . I am not sure . . ."

"Your Percy will be Fey or Knight, Lady. That is the choice God gives you."

"Never Knight! Never Knight!" Alanna kissed the soft, fuzzy head nuzzled in her neck. *Have I not seen enough of the virtue and Honor that breed endless Death, circling like ravens?* "Edik, I will go! I will take Percy to the Fey forest!"

"Whisper, Lady."

"Ah, yes." But no one had heard. The dusky room beyond Edik was empty.

Brightly eager now, Alanna turned to Ivie. "You will come, Ivie? Had I been offered this chance when I was young . . ."

But Alanna stopped there. When she was young she had been virtuous, honorable. She had always done as she was told. Her braid, now greying, had been a dark, rich brown, like fertile soil; never tinged with the fire of self-will, like Ivie's braid.

Is this truly a good choice for Ivie?

Till a moment ago Ivie had no choice. She faced rough old Sir Ryan's bed, repeated childbirths, likely death in childbirth; and there was no escape. Now . . .

After all, who knows what may await in the Fey forest? Magic castles? Frog princes? Maybe a truly better life!

"You can stay here and wed Sir Ryan if—"

"I'd go to Hell first, if I knew the way!"

"Not so far," Edik said gently. "But fast. They are saying down in the hall that Sir Ryan rides here now."

Holy Mary! And me just up from childbed, and all of forty years old!

All the same. "Edik, we will go with you."

"Tomorrow night, then. Before the moon flowers full."

Edik pulled his donkey up on a dark edge of forest. He turned to Alanna and Ivie, reining in behind him, and said very softly, "Ladies, this is your last chance to turn back."

The four donkeys huddled together, waggling nervous ears and shaking heads. One was laden with the little baggage Edik had allowed to be packed. ("Take only what you can carry, walking.") The only exception, Alanna's wooden Mary statue, lay strapped along the donkey's back. Alanna would not leave her garden without that. Down the donkey's sides bulged two sacks of tools and cook pots wrapped in clothes. Nothing clinked or jangled. For two nights they had traveled silent but for soft hoof-beats, muffled in soft earth.

Crossing the last pasture the second evening, they had steered toward the full moon hanging over the Forest ahead, the full moon which, for some reason, Edik considered so important. But now they had come to the forest edge; in forest shadow, the moon was hidden behind trees.

Last chance to turn back?

Saddle-sore, bleeding and exhausted, Alanna was tempted.

She looked over at Ivie; at swaddled Percy, held against her shoulder. (If Alanna held him, he wanted to nurse continually. At Ivie's breast, he slept.) Dressed as a peasant boy, exuberant hair hidden inside her tunic, Ivie glowed in the dark. So excited, so rejoicing to be free was Ivie, *If I said "turn back," she would go on in by herself!*

And God and Mary know, we have fled. We have deserted hall and King and Sir Ryan Ironside already. How to explain our absence, should we turn back now?

And my babe there, sleeping on Ivie's shoulder; Knight he must never be! Nothing has changed.

Edik dismounted and came to help Alanna. She could almost step to ground off the little donkey; yet with the encumbrance of gown, pain and modesty, dismounting took a few awkward moments. By the time she stood squarely, looking up at budding trees and into dark forest depths, Ivie was on her feet jiggling whimpering Percy; and herself a-jiggle, wildly eager to enter their new, mysterious life.

Edik murmured, "If you are sure, I'll unpack the donkey."

"Aye," Alanna told him firmly, quietly, "we're sure."

She studied the darkness ahead. *A new life awaits us here. Edik warned us it would not be easy. My own soul warned me. I have worked hard all my life. Now I will need to work harder than ever, and watch out for our defense. Ivie and I will be entirely responsible for our-*

selves—and for Percy—from now on forever. Amen, so be it.

"Ladies, I am turning the donkeys loose."

"What?"

"Turning the donkeys loose. Since you are determined."

Alanna turned to Edik. He had the baggage on the ground. Mary stood by Herself on Her feet like a fifth person, a near-grown child. "Surely, not all the donkeys."

"Yes, all."

"But Edik, how will you return to the hall?"

"I will not return."

Edik stepped from one donkey to the next, slapping each lightly on the rump. In no rush, the donkeys ambled a short way and stopped to graze.

I should have realized . . . Edik could no more explain our absence—and his—then we could!

"But do you mean to enter the Fey forest, yourself?"

"Even so." Very calm, Edik scanned the sky above the trees.

"But you said . . . once in, we can never come out!"

"That is the rule."

"Edik!" Alanna's thankful astonishment overflowed; two or three tears coursed down her cheeks. "You carry loyalty too far!"

"Not so, Lady. Not so at all. Don't weep. You'll need clear eyes for this night's work."

"I cannot believe . . ."

"I do this for myself, Lady."

"For yourself?" Alanna dried her eyes on her sleeve.

"Now Sir Ogden is gone and you are content with your choice, nothing holds me to this land. I may as well make myself a new life, even as you do."

"Ah . . ." *Edik wants a new life?*

"Twenty-five years I have lived to serve. Now I am free. And remember, Lady. Once we enter this forest, I owe you no further service."

"I understand." *With difficulty.*

"You cannot understand yet, but you will. In there, all are equal."

He's right; it is a hard thought. All equal!

"Mark me. Any service I do you there, I will do only for love." Still, Edik scanned the sky.

"I understand."

"Once you set foot under those trees, Lady, your life, your being, will change forever."

Take a deep breath!

"Aha!"

Alanna lifted her eyes to the treetops.

There rose the full moon, a silver grail.

Thump! Thump-thump!

"Edik!" Startled Alanna croaked. "What is that sound?"

Percy thrashed briefly in Ivie's grip. Ivie swayed like a windblown birch and joggled him.

Thump! Thump-thump!

"That drum will beat all night. That is why we can enter the forest, almost safely, on this one night."

"What . . . who . . ."

"Good Folk beat that drum."

"Holy Mary!"

"I can still catch a donkey for you."

"Oh . . . no. No." Faintly, Alanna reminded herself, "Never, never, Knight!"

"Then follow in my footsteps. Now is the time. Stay in tree-shadow. Out of moonlight. Ivie, will Percy be quiet?"

"When we move, he'll be quiet."

"One moment more."

Facing forest and drum, Edik raised and swept his arms about.

A signal.

He let his arms sink, and sighed deeply. "There. Now, we move." He shouldered a small sack, one he himself had added to the load, unnoticed. Turning to wooden Mary, he caught Her about the waist and lifted Her in his arms like a heavy child.

Edik strode forward.

With no breath of hesitation, Ivie skipped after him.

The baggage! Clothes, tools, cook pots!

Edik disappeared into the night forest.

Alanna gathered up the three sacks. She slung one sack over her shoulder, and clutched two with one fist. At the new weight, she bled harder. Burdened and bleeding, she struggled into forest shadow.

Moonlight struck down between great trunks. That fluttering movement ahead must be Ivie, with now-silent Percy.

Slowly, painfully, Alanna skirted moonlight from

tree to tree. Each tree passed was a new barrier placed forever between Percy and Knighthood. At first she glanced back often toward the open, silvering space left behind. Quickly it shrank between trunks, behind fern and bracken, and disappeared.

Flitting, stumbling, they passed one distant drum, and approached another. Far to the side, they could hear yet a third far, faint drum.

This is a new world. Who said it would be better than the old? Only Edik. Why was I so eager to believe it?

Too late to wonder, now.

Tree by tree, shadow by shadow, Alanna passed into mystery.

Before they built their own bower, Alanna and Ivie built Mary's bower. On Edik's advice, She stood by the trail they soon trampled from their small, sunny clearing down to the river. He said, "She will help keep you safe." Alanna never doubted it.

Edik showed them how to bend saplings over Her, and weave branches and rushes between; and they used this same method to build their own shelter. Only, with his help, they made it stronger.

Edik found them seeds—they never asked where— and they spaded the clearing and planted peas and onions against the winter.

Edik had said, "Any service I do you there, I will do only for love." Alanna chose not to wonder, nor to question the love that moved Edik to help them build their bower; to show them new methods of fishing and trapping; to teach them which wild plants and mushrooms to eat, and which to avoid; and to bring them meat.

She was only glad that Edik never suggested sharing the bower he had helped build. He came and went, appeared and disappeared like a songbird, or like a Fey; quietly, she and Ivie rejoiced in this.

Alanna found herself calling him Sir Edik. At first she said this only when speaking with Ivie. Then, one day, the "Sir" slipped out in conversation with him.

She blushed warmly and stepped back away. *Maybe he did not hear . . . maybe he will ignore . . .*

He turned to her, startled, pleasure bright in his face. "Have I been knighted, Alanna?"

Confused, surprised at herself, Alanna explained slowly to both of them. "I . . . I knight you myself, Sir Edik. For what that's worth."

"I'd rather you than Arthur, High King! But why?"

"Because . . . because you have shown me such good courtesy!" *More courtesy than Sir Ogden ever did!* "You do not object?"

He laughed. "I do not object! But how will you explain that 'Sir' to Percy, as he grows? You don't want him to know about Sirs!"

"Oh, Percy! Percy will simply take it for your name."

"Then so do I, Alanna. With thanks."

Percy commenced loud and demanding, and grew more so. He kept Alanna and Ivie both running to rescue him several times a day. Sir Edik made him a basket, in which they laid him down to sleep as they tried to work at their new skills. But their main task continued to be changing moss diapers, feeding, bathing and entertaining Percy.

More than once, Ivie sighed. "If we were back at the hall now, Percy Lamb would have a nurse."

"And you would have a husband."

"Mary and Martha! I forgot!"

"That's why you came out here."

"But you know, Lady, a nurse wouldn't run to Percy every time he bawled! She would have other things to do, even as we have here. She would swaddle him tight against his cradleboard and leave him to yowl."

"And she would not worry that his yowls might call interested . . . Others . . . to him."

Ivie signed the Cross on her forehead and shoulders, and then on Percy's.

Their first fears of the Fey had calmed, somewhat. Always they watched with wide-open eyes—in their clearing, on the trails they made to the stream, to their traps and wild herb patches. Using all viligance, they saw no Fey. No Good Folk appeared. And only the drums that throbbed on full-moon nights reminded them that this forest was Fey.

Sir Edik explained the drums. "When the moon flowers, the Good Folk dance and mate."

"Mate?"

"Like pagans at Midsummer fires."

Evil walks when the moon flowers—I mean, when the moon is full. Then Satan rules his forest. Holy Mary defend!

Alanna issued her first command. "We must all be

safely inside the bower by the first drumbeat, and stay there till sunrise!"

She meant, all four of them. But when she turned to Sir Edik, he had vanished.

By midsummer Alanna and Ivie settled into a routine. They gardened, fished and trapped, taking turns with Percy's constant care. While learning new skills, they had lost their former major occupation. "It feels so strange," Ivie said once, "to never spin, or weave, or sew!"

Alanna agreed. "Any time my hands are idle they reach for distaff and spindle."

"At this rate, Lady, we'll soon be wearing skins." The clothes they had brought were showing serious wear.

"I wonder where we will find skins!"

"I know where."

Alanna also knew where.

When they first set up housekeeping in the clearing, wild creatures avoided it. Slowly, they drifted back in. Dawn and dusk, small roe deer browsed around Mary's bower. Sir Edik suggested guarding the peas with a line of evil scent—filthy clothes, Percymoss, even feces. Alanna shuddered. But Ivie took his advice. The stink worked, more or less.

Once a red fox appeared among the peas, pouncing here and there on dormice. He paused to watch Alanna and Ivie with interested, curious eyes, even as they watched him. Satisfied they were harmless, he went back to his hunting. "We'll have more peas for that!" Alanna said happily. "Fewer mice, more peas! How can we lure him back here?" But they never saw him again.

Once a wildcat crept up on Percy where he lay in his basket in the shade. Ivie and Alanna had turned both their backs in the garden; but Percy's roars brought them both running in time. The wildcat paused, hissed, then streaked away into a thicket.

Rocking Percy to sleep in her arms that night, Alanna whispered, "Ivie, have you thought? That cat might as well have been . . ."

"Lady! Shush!" Ivie swiveled frightened eyes toward the dusky bower entrance.

But Alanna could not shush. Whispers and murmurs spilled over from her rising fountain of fear. "You know, I have sometimes wondered if *they* might want to steal Percy. *They* do steal babes, that is known."

Watching the doorway, Ivie agonized. "Lady! Hush!"

"And I have wondered if *they* might come in the night, any night, and cut our throats while we dream. But as yet we have seen no hair, no whisker—"

"I have!"

"What?" Alanna stared through deep, indoor dusk into Ivie's wide, fear-glinting eyes. "What have you seen?"

"I think. Yesterday."

"In Mary's holy name! What?"

"As I brought water from the river . . ."

Alanna leaned nose to nose with Ivie. She breathed, "Speak, girl!"

"At the steep place in the trail . . . no breath left in me . . . I thought I saw . . . something . . ." Ivie made a graceful, bounding hand gesture. "Like that. Cross the trail ahead of me."

Hopefully, "Squirrel? Hare?"

"Two legs."

"Aaahh . . ."

"Brown breeches. Tunic. Cap."

"How big?"

"Maybe like a . . . wolfhound.

"Mary defend!"

A few days passed; then Alanna, standing carefully among prickly blackberry vines, felt . . . watched.

She had grown used to this feeling in the forest. Eyes watched, always and everywhere—bird eyes, mouse eyes. Maybe wolf eyes.

But this time, she paused in her work. With purple-stained, bleeding fingers she dropped three plump blackberries into the reed basket slung from her neck. Then she stood like wooden Holy Mary, feeling the forest around her.

Sunlight slanted down between giant oak trunks into the blackberry clearing. Birds chirped and hopped in branches high and low. A dormouse perched on a blackberry tip, still as herself, watching her. She looked back at it. Thought, *It's not you. Not you I feel . . .*

The watching came from . . . she felt it most strongly on her left side.

Quickly, abruptly, she turned her head.

And saw only green and golden light; orange and brown oak trunks.

She looked lower.

There.

Alanna breathed in, and not out again.

Down among blackberry vines, knee-high to Alanna, brown eyes gazed up at her.

The eyes were set close together in a small, brown face; the curious, interested gaze reminded her of the fox in the peas.

Black braids poked from under a dun skin cap to brush frail shoulders. Mouth and chin were purple. With dried blood? No. *Blackberry juice.*

The mouth gaped briefly. Fox-sharp incisors peeked out.

Alanna struggled to breathe.

The face vanished.

No leaf moved.

Alanna let go her breath and gasped in huge, new breath.

The face was gone. But its image hung still in her eyes, branded upon her mind. Again she saw juice-dark mouth, foxy eyes and teeth.

Was only curious. Meant no harm. This time.

Alanna drew breath again. And remembered—

—*Percy! Holy, blessed Mary!*

Percy was back at the bower with Ivie. Probably in his basket. Probably outdoors. Probably cooing and gurgling so the woods around resounded. Ivie would be trying to work—scrape a skin? braid reeds? pull a weed? Ivie might turn her back!

Alanna crossed herself.

Frozen life flowed again up and down her body.

Heedless of clinging prickles, she tore herself out of the vines. Ran straight into an oak where she expected a trail. Spun around. Found the trail. Bounded along it like a hare.

Wrong way. Wrong trail. *Have to go back to the blackberry clearing with the little brown thing . . .*

Mary and Martha, they're all around! Makes no difference. They're laughing at me now.

She clung to a birch, seeing this. Understanding. Accepting.

Breathless, she ran back up the trail to the blackberries.

Found the right trail. Trotted home gasping, hands pressed to aching breast and side.

Trees and shade gave way.

There stood the bower in full sunshine. Alone. Fearfully exposed. Its solid-woven back to Alanna.

She staggered out into the open. Across to the bower. Around the bower. Every labored breath now a loud agony.

Ivie sat cross-legged in the shadowed entrance. She had laid her reed-braiding aside to hold three-month-old Percy upright between her knees. They laughed together, Ivie softly, Percy crowing like a rooster. Alanna had not heard his crowing through her own rasping, tearing breath.

Now they heard her gasps. Two human faces turned to her. They were safe, alive. Both of them.

Alanna caught hold of the bower's wicker frame and hung from it, panting.

Percy yelled joyful greetings and held out his arms.

Ivie's jaw dropped. Blue eyes widened.

She said only, "Where's your berry basket?"

Alanna could not yet speak to answer.

"You had a berry basket," Ivie reminded her. "Hung on your neck. Percy and I, we were just talking about those berries."

Percy jumped up and down in Ivie's scarred, hardened hands.

Alanna looked at her own hands. Purple. Scummy. She must have been picking berries.

Aye. I was picking berries. And then . . .

She sank down beside Ivie. Took eager Percy into her lap. Bared breast for him.

She said, "I saw . . . I saw . . ."

Ivie's eyes widened yet farther.

"Cap . . . fox eyes . . ."

Firmly, softly, Ivie said, "Hush."

Again, a few days. Then Alanna led the way up the bank and home from the sunset-tinged river. They had bathed Percy. Alanna had wished to bathe, herself; but then she thought of the little brown fox-face in the blackberries and clutched her ragged gown close.

She went first, brave hand on the knife at her hip. Ivie followed with clean, wide-awake Percy in her arms. Shadows deepened ahead. *Better get home fast . . . no dawdling . . . no being out in the woods at night . . .*

Alanna slowed, and stopped in shadow. Ivie stopped behind her. Percy jumped impatiently in her arms.

It's only my fear, showing itself. Only my shivers.

Red slanting sunlight pooled between two pines ahead. Did a quiet figure stand in that light?

Alanna gripped her knife hilt. *It's a trick of light. And my shivers.*

Percy fussed louder.

Must get home!

Alanna stepped forward. Stopped again.

Holy Mary, it's real!

The figure raised a greeting hand, palm forward, and took clear shape. A small, dark lady stood in the trail. From under a crown of wildflowers her long, black braid dropped down her long, embroidered gown. Black as her braid, her keen eyes met Alanna's with a . . . kind . . . glance.

Behind Alanna, Ivie gasped.

Alanna planted herself like a tree between the small, kind lady and Percy.

The lady smiled—slowly, carefully, showing no tooth. But Alanna guessed at hidden, fox-sharp incisors. She drew her knife halfway from its sheath.

Haltingly, with strange inflections, the lady said, "I Lady of Lake. Nimway. All know I." Her gentle, husky voice froze Alanna's hand on the knife.

The lady said, "I let you come. Guard you. No harm. Yes."

She moved from red light into shadow. Stepped

closer. And close, raising her eyes to hold Alanna's own.

Alanna tried to grip the knife hilt. *I'm falling asleep! Can't move!*

Couldn't fight, anyway. She's not here alone! There's little skin-capped men behind every tree, pointing poisoned darts at us.

Her numb fingers slept on the knife hilt.

The Lady of the Lake stopped before Alanna. Smiled up at her, close-mouthed. Looked past her.

Alarm tingled up Alanna's spine as those deep, keen eyes fell on Percy behind her. *If I could move! Must move!*

Despairing, *She doesn't need men with poisoned darts. She is her own army.*

Behind Alanna, Percy suddenly cooed and laughed.

Soft, friendly, the lady said, "Greetings, Percival. Never-Knight-To-Be."

ALANNA'S COUNSEL

God makes men and men make rules
So we know Knights from baser fools.
If in truth you'd be a Knight,
Keep these counsels in your sight.
Should you meet a maiden fair,
Kiss her well and leave her there.
Take her jewels if you must.
Use no violence nor lust.
Should God's church stand by your way,
Enter there and gravely pray.
Guard your Honor and your Word.
A Knight's Word is his Spirit's sword.
Accept a friendly gift of food
In jovial and friendly mood.
If none is offered, fill your need.
Of angry protests take no heed.
Upon your way you hear a cry?
Answer it! Help, save, or die!
Should Another challenge you,
Take sword or lance and run him through.
Follow faithfully your King
So Merlin may your praises sing.
Now my Counsel's said and done;
All I can give you, dear Sir Son.

3

Red Knight

In a bright, morning glade shone a large, silvery tent.

Stepping out of the woods, Percy paused.

"Goddamn! What we could do with a tent like that back in the forest!"

Behind him, still woods-shadowed, Lili murmured, "Too seeable. Stands out like a white cliff. I wouldn't sleep long enough to dream in that!"

On three sides woods framed the glade. Spring-green leaves shimmered and birdsong echoed. On the farside open fields stretched away, green and brown. A grey, grizzled horse grazed in the first field, hobbling on three legs. One front leg was tied up off the ground.

In the midst, obvious and direct, the tent flew a cheerful red and blue banner. Bright ribbons snapped and floated on a light breeze. The tent flap hung invitingly open. A smaller tent, unadorned, waited off to the side.

Percy said, "I know! This must be a church of God." In his head a despairing voice moaned, *Should God's church stand by your way, enter there . . .*

He made to start forward. But Lili's small, clenched fist shot up before his nose. *Wait!*

Why?

Lili doubled down and darted out across the open, grassy glade. Straight to the smaller tent she went, and hesitated, sniffing, listening.

She vanished. *Went in, she did. Good thought. Know what we're getting into.*

There she came now, slipping out through the still-closed tent flap. She raised her hands and finger-talked across the sunny space. *Empty. But look at the ground!*

The ground. *Ho, what a mess! Crushed grass. Churned earth. Turds all over. Great horse turds, dog turds. There's one, steaming. Human folk have been around here, and not long back.* Percy signed, *Well, aye. We Human folk go to church. Now watch me!*

Percy straightened Alanna's soup kettle on his head. He threw back his cloak to flaunt his new, three-colored tunic. Lightly, he touched the Bee Sting at his belt. Assured and ready, he marched across the glade, avoiding turds, and into the church.

Hey?

In a church they've got an altar, like a table. A lamp, always lit. Maybe a statue, like Mary.

Here, they've got a table. Spread with every kind of food known, and other kinds, unknown. Goddamn!

Lo; this is not God's church.

Small furniture stood about; wooden things to sit on; a chest to keep things in; and furs and coverlets piled up to form a bed.

On the bed slept a lady. *A maiden fair.*

Except not so fair.

Must be Ivie's age. Best thing she's got is her hair.

Which was dark, long, rich, and thickly spread across embroidered pillows.

Should you meet a maiden fair, kiss her well . . .

Percy bent down over the lady.

How? Cheek? Forehead? How do you turn your head . . . There.

He landed a heavy, wet kiss on her upturned chin. *????*

The lady's eyes flew open. Saw Percy. The lady drew a great breath and made to rise.

But Percy knew what that meant.

Think you'll scream, do you? Not in my ear! I've heard enough of that.

Percy silenced the lady with one hand firm on her mouth. With the other hand he held her down by a slim shoulder.

Black eyes wide on his, she raised both bony little hands against his chest.

Rings. Bright rings winked pretty colors on every finger, even the thumbs.

Take her jewels if you must.

Rings are jewels.

Cautiously, he lifted his hand from her mouth. She took a quiet breath and watched him.

Carefully, he let go of her shoulder. She lay still and watched him.

He took one little bony hand and pulled off the

rings, finger by finger. She gasped a bit when a ring stuck; otherwise, she lay silent.

There. Like that, In the pouch. Now the other hand. She says no "nay." I must be doing it right.

Holy Michael, I'm hungry! That food back there smells right good.

Percy rose up from the lady and turned to the table.

Lili was already there, stuffing bread into her pouch.

Accept a friendly gift of food . . . If none is offered, fill your need . . .

He made for the table and filled his need.

Breads. Meats, fish, fowl, and something like bread but honeysweet. Hungry Percy wolfed.

Lili snatched three or four sweets and returned to her watch-out post by the entrance.

A good girl, my Lili. Useful.

Following her example, Percy stuffed honeycakes into his pouch with the rings. *Never tasted the like of these!*

A rustle of movement behind him. He turned to face the lady.

Slowly, making no sudden move, she sat up on the bed; licked her lips, and asked softly, "Sirrah? Knave? Fellow?"

Percy informed her through a big mouthful of fowl. "Sir."

"Sir! Ha! Ha-ha-ha!"

Unaccountable laughter. Chewing, he stared.

"Very well. Sir; my lord has gone hunting."

"M-hmmm." Nod.

"He will return soon. With his men."

"M-hmmm?" Chew. Gulp down.

"He will be angry."

Angry? Why?

"What are you, a beggar?"

What's that? Shrug. Tear off a hunk of pork.

"You are not a peddler . . . Oh!" Her plain little face lit up. Excitement turned it almost pretty. "A bard! Sir, are you a bard?"

Could she not see? "Knight am I." Pop in the pork.

"Ha-ha-ha!" She shook pretty black hair back over her shoulders. Cocked her head. "I know! You're a jester! A fool! My lord sent you here."

Percy scowled.

"You're good. But rough for my taste. A soup kettle makes a good helmet, I admit. But where's your sword?"

Percy gestured toward his Bee Sting.

This big flagon here, does it hold horrible milk, or water?

With both hands Percy lifted, tipped and quaffed.

UGH! Neither milk nor water, it burned his tongue, then his throat, and all the way down to his stomach. Gingerly, he ran tongue over teeth, testing the awful aftertaste. Still, he was thirsty; so he drank again, more slowly.

"Easy on the ale, Sir Jester. My lord likes his ale."

From the entrance, Lili said, "Percy, get one of those warm covers and let's be gone."

Percy let the flagon fall. He wiped the taste off

his lips and looked at the embroidered coverlets on the bed.

"Hard to carry."

"I'll carry it." Lili disappeared outside.

Percy strode to the bed. The blue and red coverlet he had his eye on lay under the lady. He took her by waist and shoulder, lifted her aside, not too urgently, and took it up.

Anger stiffened her face and turned it plain again. Homely.

Coldly, she asked, "Who is that boy?"

"My friend. We travel together."

"Travel? You are traveling?"

"Aye, this moment. Farewell."

"I assure you, my lord will avenge this robbery! He will hunt you down like a wolf."

He could try. Percy shrugged.

"Leave the coverlet. Then maybe he will only break all your bones."

Percy slung the coverlet back over his shoulder. Lili might regret offering to carry this! But it would cheer up a cold night.

"Would you know the name of your doom?"

Turning to leave, he looked back inquiringly.

"For the rest of your short life, beware of Sir Agrain. He is unusually fierce."

Percy left the tent.

Lili had already vanished. A very faint dew-trail led into the woods.

Out in the field, the grey-grizzled horse whinnied. Percy paused to look at it. It looked back at him, head and hobbled foot high, ears waggling. It whinnied again.

Take the horse?

In the past two days since leaving the forest they had met several horsemen and groups of horsemen. When they could, they hid till the travelers had passed; for Lili feared them greatly. And Percy noticed that Humans sometimes hid from them, also. There must be some reason for all this caution.

From thicket or tree they had watched the big animals jog past, hooves splattering stones, riders alert, commanding, yet relaxed, their lucky feet up and off the stony ground.

Once, unable to hide, they had stood by the trail and watched powerful horses pass close by, great hooves threatening, hides smelling of sweat, hot breath smelling of hay.

Percy had thought, *Goddamn! That's how to travel! Take the horse!*

But how?

How would you approach it? Gaze high and scornful, it dared Percy.

Not one to refuse a challenge, Percy started for it. It hobbled away at his own speed. When he stopped it stopped, and looked back at him.

Suppose I caught it, how would I get on?

It wore no furniture such as the riders used; nothing to sit on. Its bare swayback glistened silver in morning sun. Nothing to guide with. It had something on its face you could catch it by, but that was all.

Lili must be far away by now. *Goddamn! She's gone into the woods.*

Over the fields was the direct way to Arthur's Dun. *But then; no Fey would walk those fields in daylight. She'll want to dodge from tree to tree all the way.*

Percy sighed. *I'm Human, that's why open fields don't fright me. Not Lili's fault that she's Fey.*

As for the horse, I'll wait till I know more.

Right now, catch up with Lili. Let her carry this coverlet. Look, she broke a twig here, and here, so I could follow.

Percy crashed into the woods on Lili's deliberately visible trail.

"Lili, Goddamn! Why can't you sleep?"

(I have to laugh.) "Why can't *you* sleep? These rocks and thorns too much for you?"

"This Goddamn itch! You said you could fix it."

"Haven't found the right herb yet."

"Doesn't bother you, huh? You Fey can sleep on rock with an itch?"

"So can you! Or you should have stayed home in your oak nest with Alanna's soft, warm cloak."

"Wish I had brought that!"

"I wish so, too. It could have done for both of us."

"She gave me her soup kettle. And her counsel."

"Which is no good, Percy. Merlin never sang of such deeds as you have done."

"Why did I never hear these Merlin songs you talk of?"

"Alanna did not want you knowing them. Percy!"

(Wide-awake, I sit up and look out of our brush shelter into rainy darkness.) "Alanna must have forgotten how it really is, out here in this Kingdom."

Groan. "Never forgot a Goddamn—"

"In the songs, the Round Table Knights take no rings or food. Their evil enemies do those things!"

"Hah! And do the Knights hand out pretty rings to the first folks they meet?"

"We Fey return good for good. Even Merlin's songs admit that. And those peasants were good to us. Had us sleep in their own bed, while they curled up by the fire!"

"That's where I caught this itch. And then you had to reward them with rings! Sir Friendly was right. Women are more trouble than worth."

(That stings!) "You want me to leave you alone out here? I can start home right now."

"Might as well wait till morning."

"Percy."

(Moan.) "What now?"

"Those peasant folks didn't know we had rings."

"What are rings for, anyhow? No good I can see. Pretty to look at. But if I had a ring now, I'd gladly give it for a dish of peasant porridge!"

"They didn't know . . . till morning."

"What are you fretting for? Lie down. Warm me up."

"All day I've been wondering why they gave us their bed."

"All day I've been wishing they hadn't!"

"I woke up in the night, Percy. I saw a Spirit hover

over them, where they lay on the ground. Something I've never seen before."

"Aaargh. You see spirits burning in every bush!"

"Not like this one. This was too bright, too great, to fit into the hut. Its wings reached the sky."

"You couldn't see the sky. We were inside the hut. Lie down!"

"All I could see was spirit and sky. The hut disappeared."

"Angel Michael! I dreamed, too, me, myself. I dreamed I was roasting a grouse."

Poor, ever-hungry Percy! "I'll find you a grouse in the morning."

"And that itch herb, too. O-o-o-ow!" (Scratch.)

I lie down again beside Percy and rearrange the coverlet over us. He cuddles warm against me; as he must have cuddled against Alanna when he was small.

What with itch, rock, rain and thorn, lovemaking is far from my mind. It has never entered Percy's mind.

And that's as well. I think that last night I glimpsed the Power I seek. That great, shining Spirit that hovered over our sleeping hosts . . . It knows the secret of Power.

Percy flings a warm, too-heavy arm over me and snores.

Why did those peasant folk welcome us into their hut, feed us porridge, give us their bed? They didn't even know we had those pretty rings to give.

Finger pressed to Victory, I stare into wet darkness and wonder.

*   *   *

Here I am!

In Arthur's Dun!

Here I stand among Human men. I am bigger, stronger, then most of them. I look upon King's Hall; upon its great doors and carved posts; and I know that King Arthur himself sits within.

Follow faithfully your King . . . Faithful I will be, whatever comes!

One barrier remains. Those great, closed doors. From what I have heard, traveling, King Arthur is not easily met with.

(While Percy worshipped at the doors of Chivalry, oblivious to the lowly Humans hurrying past and around, Lili cowered in his shadow, almost too frightened to breathe. So close she clung, few of those hasty Humans noticed her at all.)

Well. Ho-so. No use standing here.

Percy squared his broad shoulders, tapped the soup kettle straight on his head and stepped forward.

A thunderous growl rumbled behind the closed doors.

Percy paused.

Like sudden wind, the growl rose into a roar. Every Human on the street stopped dead and turned to face King's Hall. Hands reached for sword hilts, knives, hammers.

Percy reached for his Bee Sting.

The roar within became a sustained racket. Men shouted. A woman screamed.

The great doors facing Percy burst open.

Out from King's Hall, as though propelled by the uproar, rushed a furious, red figure.

From under a red helmet bushed red hair and beard. A red cloak flowed down over red cuirass and surcoat. The red-gloved right hand clapped sheathed sword hilt close; in his left hand the Red Knight bore a large cup grail.

An instant he paused. His grim gaze darted over the street and stopped on Percy's gape. It took in Percy's soup-kettle helmet and three-colored tunic.

The Red Knight strode to Percy. Held out the yellow-gleaming grail.

"You, Knave. Take this grail."

Knave? Wait a moment, here—

"Go you in there. Give that to the Queen. I took it from her. Give the King this message." The Red Knight's inflamed eyes fixed Percy. "This message, Sirrah. *Give me back my lands, or send one to fight me for them. I wait without.* You can remember that?"

"Sir, I am not a messenger—"

"You'll do! God's teeth, the Queen will love you! Now say to me your message. *Give me back my lands . . .* Say it!"

(Lili pinched Percy in the back.)

I am not a messenger. I never thought to enter King's Hall with a message!

(Lili punched Percy.)

Lo! This message is for the King. Giving this message, I can reach the King's side!

Percy repeated the message. "*Give me back my lands or send one to fight for them. I wait without.*"

"Go in, fellow. Do your part. Remember, I wait
without! If no one comes out to fight, I will go raise
me an army. Tell the King that." And the Red Knight
shouted past Percy to someone in the street, "My
horse, fool! To me, here!"

A cloud of joy steamed from the gleaming grail up
into Percy's face. *With this, I speak to the King! Instantly!*

Holding the precious grail two-handed before him,
as though it might spill its joyful promise, Percy
stepped past the Red Knight. He entered the great
doors of King's Hall just as men came from within
to close them. They glanced at his outfit and moved
to bar his way. They saw the grail he carried and
stood away back. Thus, did Percy enter King's Hall.
(And thus, close on his heels as his shadow, did Lili.)

Percy had formed no idea in his head of what
King's Hall should be like inside. Yet he felt that
something was not right here. The storm of shouts
and curses was echoed around the hall by overturned
benches, chairs, stools. Food, hurled around the floor,
squelched under Percy's boots. Wolfhounds were
making short work of it. Men who had just leaped
up, overturning chairs, stood shouting around a huge
round table.

These men are all unarmed! Where are the Knights?
Where is the King?

Percy looked from angry face to astonished face to
gleefully amused face. No King here!

(Lili tugged on his hair, raising his face.)

Up there. Beyond the round table.

Two great, carved chairs occupied a dais, one

lower than the other. On the lower chair slumped a slender, red-haired woman. Alanna-like, she had fainted. On the higher chair—

The King.

Arthur sat quiet, straight and calm. A narrow crown circled his dark, greying hair. On the wall beside him hung his shield, emblazoned with Mary's image; and his magic sword.

Percy strode past the round table to the dais. On the way, he felt Lili vanish away from behind him.

Close, he saw that the King's hands, which seemed to rest on his robed knees, were clenched and white-knuckled.

Closer, he saw the Queen open her eyes. Some powerful feeling had drained her face pure white. Her rich gown was drenched as though by heavy rain; and bits of meat and bread mingled with pretty jewels down her front.

Her instantly angry eye lit on the grail in Percy's two hands.

She jerked upright and stretched a dripping, ringed hand for it.

Percy was making straight for the King. But now the Red Knight spoke in his head. *Give that to the Queen. I took it from her.*

First this message.

Hardly pausing, he thrust the grail into the Queen's hand.

Now for the real one.

The King's calm, grey eyes had watched this exchange of the grail. His hands remained clenched and white on his knees. No muscle stirred. With mild half interest, he gave Percy his attention.

This is the King who shall knight me!

Percy cleared his throat. Loudly, he said, "Sir! The Red Knight outside asked me to say this to you."

Interest quickened in the royal eyes.

"This is his message, Sir, not mine." *Better make that clear.*

The King nodded.

"This way it goes. 'Give me back my lands or send one to fight for them. I wait without. If no one comes out to fight, I will go raise me an army.' Those, Sir, are the Red Knight's words."

The King stood up from his chair.

Tall he is, big, like me! How his jeweled robe gleams! and his rings! Next time I take a fair maiden's rings I will keep them!

The King raised both ringed hands, palms out, over the crowd below the dais. As though a giant hand had covered its mouth, King's Hall fell suddenly silent. Percy felt the gaze of all eyes pass through him and fasten on King Arthur.

Arthur's great voice rang through Percy and around the Hall. "The Red Knight demands a fight for his lands. He waits without."

Voices murmured, "Not you, Lord!"

"Why fight? You have his lands!"

"I'll fight him!"

"Me, Lord! I'll go!"

A big, dark man, unarmed like the rest, sprang onto the dais beside Percy. "With these eyes I saw him snatch the Queen's grail and dash ale in her face! Gladly I'll avenge that deed, and win his lands as well."

A shout went up at that. "Aye! Let Sir Lancelot settle it! In a trice!"

Percy's stumbling mind reeled, straightened up, stood square. *So that's the way of it! Goddamn, here's my chance!*

"Sir," he shouted above the rising voices. "Sir! I will fight the Red Knight for you! I, Sir Percival."

The King turned almost-startled eyes back to Percy.

The Queen and Sir Lancelot stared.

Behind the dais, a girl laughed.

Laughing, she stepped out from Arthur's shadow.

Percy watched only the King's face. But he saw from a corner of his eye that she was black-haired, small and slender in a white gown, and that she laughed close-mouthed, like Lili.

At her laugh King's Hall fell silent again. Into this new silence she said clearly, "Lord! Never will your Round Table boast a knight greater than this Sir Percival."

Percy's heart swelled, burst, flamed. Joyful pride burned hot and high. *Goddamn!*

"Sir! I go to fight your enemy."

Percy swung about and marched down from the dais, through the crowd, to the doors.

He was almost aware of hands reached to catch him, feet outstretched to trip him, voices exclaiming. He passed through invincible, unstoppable, right hand on the Bee Sting under his cloak, and strode out into the sunny street.

There waited the Red Knight. A sword gleamed in his right hand. A shield hung on his left arm.

Beside the knight waited his horse, a great red charger furnished all in red. Restlessly, it pawed sparks from the stone pavement.

The Red Knight turned toward Percy. Looking beyond Percy, he raised his shield.

Percy stalked toward him.

The Red Knight lowered shield. "You again, clown? What message this time?"

Percy advanced upon him, hidden dart ready in his fingers, eyes on the Red Knight's eyes.

"Ho! God's teeth! What do you—"

Percy came on.

The Red Knight punched his sword hilt into Percy's left side.

Percy gasped. Did not flinch. Drove the poisoned dart through the Red Knight's left eye. Stepped back away.

The Red Knight stood amazed. Swayed. Staggered three steps back and crashed on the stone pavement.

A few gasps, a twitch. *Dead in a trice.*

Percival turned. Looked about him.

Before King's Hall crowded the unarmed men. They must have followed on his heels. They gaped, pointed, murmured. Percival barely heard their comments.

"How was that done?"

"But he was a Knight!"

"Arthur's enemy."

"True. But a Knight."

"Insulted Gwenevere."

"Still. Shouldn't die at the hands of a beggar!"

"Seize him!"

"Arm up first."

"He's unarmed! Couldn't get into the hall, armed."

"He's somehow armed. Killed him somehow."

"Weirdness here."

"Maybe magic."

"Aye," said the girl's calm voice. "Magic it must be. Leave it to me."

The growling knights stepped aside to let the small, white-robed girl through.

Straight to Percy she came, and smiled close-mouthed up into his face.

Small, she is!

She said, "Percival, this red horse and armor are now yours."

Percival stared down into her wise, dark eyes. *I've seen this girl before. Don't know where . . .*

What'd she say? Horse and armor? Horse and armor?

He whirled to look again at his victim. The corpse still twitched. Meant nothing. *He's dead. And I get the armor!*

The girl said, "Lose no time."

The gang of unarmed Knights milled and seethed like a torrent ready to flood its banks.

"Take sword and shield," she said. "Helmet. No time for the rest."

She herself seized the great, red charger's bridle.

Percival darted to the dead Red Knight. Glanced once into the astonished dead eyes. Quickly then, with his knife he cut the helmet's thongs. He tossed his soup kettle clattering, and donned the red helmet.

Heavy!

He jerked the shield off one dead arm, grabbed up the sword.

Goddamn! How's a man walk around like this?

Behind him the girl said, "Quick, get the sheath."

That meant the whole belt. In a hasty daze Percival dropped shield and sword to work the belt clasp.

The charger's great hooves rang on stone as it fought the girl's grasp. How could she hold it, small as she was? The Knights' angry buzzing grew louder, closer.

But they're all unarmed.

Right. They hesitated, milling like disturbed bees.

Feared of me!

Or of the girl?

Percival dragged the belt out from under the dead man, clasped it over his own belt. Thrust sword into sheath. With snort and clatter, the red charger came up beside him, girl still firmly in charge. Alarming, close horse scent swamped Percival's senses.

"Mount quickly. Up!"

Percival looked up the quivering red hide. Away, afar up there, Lili looked down on him. Her little face was stiff with terror.

Right before her sat a high, polished red saddle. A stirrup dangled at Percival's hand.

"Up!"

Percival had never happened to see how one mounted a horse. The horsemen whom he had watched from hiding were already up there.

The girl breathed between clenched teeth, "Foot in stirrup. Up! Up and over!"

The charger pawed and tossed its head. Froth foamed from its jaws. The girl barely hung on to its bridle. Percival saw her murmur to it, as to him.

The shield . . . how do I hold . . .

"Give Lili."

With effort, Percival handed the shield away up to Lili. Could she hold it? It came not back down.

A poke from the white-robed girl, and he was in the stirrup. Hanging between sky and pavement.

"Leg over, Percival!"

He was in the saddle.

"Reins."

Dizzily he leaned to collect the reins the girl handed up.

Behind him, the Knights roared.

Faintly, Percival felt Lili's hands grasp his belt through the cloak. He himself grabbed at the horse's tough, red mane.

The white-robed girl spoke to the charger. And let go the bridle.

Strength rushed through the huge red body below Percival.

He found himself whirled around, looking down from a new height upon the massed Knights of the Round Table. Angry faces glared up at him but an instant, then disappeared from sight.

At the doors of King's Hall stood King Arthur, sword in hand. Percival caught surprise on the royal face. Then that, too, vanished.

Undistinguished men scattered now before the on-rushing charger. Women snatched children out of its path. Huts and houses joggled past at undreamed-of speed. *Clatter-Clash* went hooves on stone street, then *thud-thump* on dirt street.

Percival clung low to the saddle. He felt Lili cling to him. Ground hurtled past as they rushed into wind.

Striding forward over rough ground, Bee Sting pounding his thigh, Percival pauses. *I've been here before.*

Here. Where? Heavy white mist rolls around even the nearest trees. All he can see is this forest-littered ground at his feet.

I've been here before; and I'm going there. (Wherever *there* may be.)

Percival springs back into stride.

I'm going there. But first, now . . . Goddamn! This is a dream, and I've dreamed it before. First, I'll see . . .

There before him it appears, dark on the ground.

As he has done before, Percival stops and looks down at the naked, Human man lying on the stretcher.

The Fisher.

Percival calls this big, blond man the Fisher because he lies on and under fishing nets, and holds a fishing spear in both helpless hands. He lies perfectly still on his back, looking up at Percival.

But . . . Angel Michael! He has the look of a King!

Studying the calm, cold face this time, Percival thinks of King Arthur. *Put a robe on him, give him a crown . . . he's not Arthur, but he's a King somewhere. How steadily he looks at me, out of his pain!*

This silent, stiff-faced man bears a bloody wound between the thighs.

As before, Percival shudders through his whole body. And looks away.

Not my hurt.

And I'm going there.

Percival steps reachingly over and across the silent Fisher King. As each time before, he strides on through mist, over rough ground, with no backward glance.

Fire leaped into darkness.

At the lord's command servants threw more kindling, more logs, into the fire pit. The fire reared and roared.

Silhouetted against the flames, two figures shambled, staggered and bear-danced, dueling with staves.

Thwack! Crack! Clonk! Their cudgels swung, crossed and landed body blows. "Arf!" "Huh!" "Hah!" grunted the two sturdy contestants.

Out beyond the light, laughter responded; shouts, comments, exhortations. Men rose from benches to crowd forward into half-light, grinning and betting.

In true darkness at the far ends of the hall, hounds snarled.

One cudgel cracked, broke. Half of it flew into the fire pit. Still gripping half, the young man ducked back from his attacker.

The winner swung his cudgel high and sideways like a fishing pole, then brought it *crack!* against the loser's head.

The loser dropped.

Whoops, guffaws and moans sounded around the hall.

The winner threw down his cudgel. He swaggered up to the lord's bench and collected his reward, a small bag of coins, with an awkward bow.

Lord Gahart grinned up at him. "Go easier next time. Good men don't grow in gardens."

"He'll fight again, Lord. His head's made of wood." The winner stepped away into winking half-light. His friends surrounded him.

Other dragged the loser up off the floor, draped his arms over two of their shoulders and half dragged him off into the dark.

Lord Gahart lifted the flagon by his side and drank. "That seems to be true," he remarked to Percival, who sat beside him. "Seen that fellow whomped before. No lasting effect. Unless maybe on the brains inside."

Robed like a lord in Gahart's own garments, Percival sat easily beside his host. Newly sophisticated, he quaffed throat-burning ale from the flagon Gahart set back down between them. A small tapestry covered their rough bench.

Never sat so soft before! Never ate so good! Even this goddamn ale's good! Here's what Human life should be!

He drank again.

"How would you like a sack of gold, Percival?"

Percival lowered the flagon, turned to Gahart.

"I'd bet on you to beat the winner. And no one else would. See?"

Hah. "You want me to fight that cudgel fellow."

"No, no! You are my honored guest. I *want* nothing from you. But if you felt like winning gold tonight," . . . Gahart drew a second small bag from his robe. "I'll bet you can."

Percival set down the flagon and made to rise. Gahart held up a meaty hand. "Not so fast! You can hardly move in that getup. You'll have to—"

"I can fight!" Percival snorted contempt for such a detail. "And I fight now this instant, Lord, or never." *Let's get this done, sit down again and finish off that ale!*

Gahart scowled.

A big man, Gahart was shorter than Percival, but three times the width, and all of it muscle. Greying red curls and beard framed a lined, scarred face. The left eye drooped.

This scowl was the first he had directed at Percival; who had seen him scowl at lesser men. He would then order beating or scourging, which his servants would promptly carry out.

Why the goddamn do they obey him? No telling who'll

be the next one flogged. But if they stood together, he could not command them.

(Lili knew no answer to this. When he asked her by lamplight in their chamber, she finger-talked, *Human ways. Your blood knows, not mine.*)

That day when the red charger went lame had been a deciding day for Percival. He did not know horses wore shoes, which could be lost. By himself, he might have eaten the charger and roamed like a beggar fool forever after. But Lili showed him what had happened. Lili brought them to Gahart's Hall and requested shelter and a horseshoe. The red charger, and Percival's red armor, had won them respect. They had both learned much, and quickly, ever since.

One thing Lili had finger-told him about Gahart. He thought of it now. Gahart's frequent anger was most dangerous against cowards and lowlies who failed to meet his smoldering eyes. Lili had signed, *If you have to, face up to him.*

Percival met Gahart's scowl with a smile. And stood up.

"Aaaagh, very well! Fight your way." Gahart rose as well. He called the startled victor away from his ale and ordered gloves and a new cudgel brought for Percival.

Servants dumped more kindling into the fire pit. The fire reared and roared. Percival faced the young victor of moments ago.

He had never held a cudgel before. Fey boys might wrestle for fun, almost never in anger. But never had he seen boys or men go at each other with sticks.

Lord Gahart's men had been showing him sword-play. This would be yet a different art.

The cudgel hung heavy, cold, in his hands. He shifted and balanced it. *How's that fellow hold his? Left hand here, right hand . . . so.*

The thwacks and *cracks* of the previous duel still sounded in his ears. *That one's strong as a plowing ox. Got to move fast. Get in there before he sees me coming.*

Percival felt a lump grow in his throat.

Then from the dark flooded a river of strength. It flowed over and around Percival and fountained within.

"Hah! Goddamn! Come on!"

Percival crouched forward; eagerly, he shook the cudgel.

The Ox grinned. Firelight gleamed in his slitted eyes and clenched teeth. He crouched, danced a few steps, raised his cudgel.

Before he sees me coming.

Percival jabbed the cudgel like a sword, under and up.

Cudgel crunched jawbone. Jaw crumbled. Teeth and blood flew.

The Ox reeled back. His cudgel crashed to the floor.

Percival sprang after him, cudgel high.

Roars from the dark.

Lord Gahart thundered, "Enough! Lay off!" Hands grabbed out of darkness and dragged Ox away.

Percival stood disappointed, swinging his blooded cudgel at air. *Never got to learn it after all.*

He felt men moving away, drawing back from heat and light, and from himself. *Never learn it now. They won't give me a chance to learn. Know I'm too good for them.*

Of a sudden, the magical strength that had supported him ebbed away. *Now I'm only me. Who was I, just now? Who was it fractured Ox's jaw?*

Lord Gahart called out, "Come get your prize, Percival!"

He stood by the tapestried bench, waving his little bag high. Laughing.

Prize. Oh, aye. Gold coins. This time I'll know to keep 'em for myself.

Percival took the bag from Gahart. A moment he hesitated, remembering Ox's awkward bow. *Should I do that?*

He sat down.

Bettors came and paid Gahart, who filled a third bag with winnings, then seated himself again by Percival. The fire wavered and sank. In gathering darkness, men wrapped themselves in cloaks and blankets and went to sleep on benches around the walls. Servants moved quietly, cleaning up. One refilled Gahart's ale flagon. Hounds roamed the floor searching out crumbs and bones.

Percival had never heard Gahart speak softly till now.

"Drink, friend. Drink."

Nothing loath, Percival drank.

"I was right to bet on you from the start. You will be a fine Knight."

"I am a fine Knight now, Lord." *Put that straight.*

"Nay, Percival. You are not yet knighted. But that day will come."

Percival wiped his lips on his embroidered sleeve. "A mage at Arthur's Dun prophesied that Arthur would have no finer knight than me."

"A mage?" Gahart took the flagon, drank, and handed it back. "Maybe he laughed when he said it?"

"She . . . long, dark hair . . . aye, she laughed. You think she joked?"

"No such thing. That which a laughing mage prophesies comes true."

"Ah." *True! Goddamn!*

"She must have been Merlin's assistant . . . Niviene."

Percival drank, and thought. *Niviene. Niviene! Of Lady Villa! Who is always away with Merlin. I was too stirred up to know her!*

A vision of Apple Island rose up out of Percival's ale-fog as if out of the misty Fey lake. He saw again the low, stony shore, ancient apple trees in bloom, a crumbling white wall of Lady Villa, groaning under vines. Behind that wall the Lady, Ivie and Alanna sat spinning. And soon Alanna would come to the door and call his child-name. "Percy? Percy! Time to go home."

He shuddered, and thrust the whole scene away, down and out of his mind. Deeply, he drank.

Niviene! Now, why didn't Lili tell me that? She's had days to tell me that!

A soft touch on his knee. Startled, he glanced down. Lili herself had come to his side and curled down like a faithful hound, cross-legged on the floor. She must have heard his thought.

Even more softly, Gahart said, "Time I learn more about you, Percival. I might maybe make plans for you."

Plans?

"You come to me from nowhere, leading that great red charger. You carry one fine red-hilted sword, one costly red shield. You wear the rags of a fool. And know no more of the world than a milk-fed brat! Do I recite the truth?"

"Aye, Lord." Though Percival winced at the description. *Still, it's true.*

"One does not ask a guest everything at once. I have waited a while to ask, but now I must know. From where did you come here, Friend Percival?"

Readily. "From Arthur's Dun. There I killed the Red Knight, Arthur's enemy. I took his horse and arms. But for some reason his enemies, Arthur's men, were angry—"

"Before that. From where did you come to Arthur's Dun?"

Another soft Lili-touch out of growing darkness.

"I came from a forest, Lord."

"A forest?"

"Aye, a forest." *No need to say what kind.* "My mother raised me there so that I would not grow up to be a Knight."

"Hah! You had no father?"

"Dead. So were my brothers dead."

"Aha. And your mother wished for you to live. But to retreat into a forest . . . she must be a bold one!"

Percival had never considered this aspect of the story. He refused to consider it now. He continued. "When she saw I would go, she told me about the world, and how to be a Knight."

Gahart spat to the side. "What could a fool woman know about that?"

Percival shrugged. "What she knew, she told me." And he began to recite. *"Should you meet a maiden fair, kiss her well and leave her there."*

Gahart grinned.

"Should God's church stand by your way, enter there and gravely pray."

Gahart laughed.

"Upon your way you hear a cry? Answer it! Help, save or die!"

Lili thumped a little fist on his knee. *Enough!*

Gahart drained the flagon and set it down on the floor. "Listen, Percival. Men do not learn from women. Women know nothing. They're just useful animals. Your red charger could tell you more of Knighthood than your mother! Knighthood must be learned from knights. Like me."

"Truth, Lord, I have learned much from you since I came here."

"I see that! You learn very fast. Now you'll learn twice as fast, because I'll show you. Tell you. Everything. That's my plan."

Percival sat speechless. *It's falling into my hands! Unasked! All of it!*

"You're wondering why."

"Aye, Lord. I wonder that very much."

"I want you for my son."

"Son?" Percival stared through near darkness into Gahart's grim face. *I've been a son. Not much joy in that.*

"You'll wed my daughter. You know the one?"

Stunned, Percival nodded. He had seen the girl about; very young and lovely, she smiled brightly to any and all. But he had noticed that Gahart's men avoided her carefully and completely. Lili had advised him to do the same.

Not that he would have kept her company by choice.

"Name's Ranna. Been saving her for someone like you."

Percival swallowed. "Saving?"

"Ranna's my only get, Percival. When I go, Ranna's all will be left of me."

Percival's mind clung to these weird words, as a fallen man clings to a cliff face.

"One day Ranna's husband will lord it in this hall. Understand?"

Slowly, Percival shook his head. ". . . Husband?"

Gahart gave a great snort. "Never wed, myself. Never was offered a chance like I'm offering you. Look. Here it is on a silver platter. I show you Knighthood. Chivalry. You go on a quest for me.

Bring back what I want. And we get the King to
knight you.

"You wed Ranna. Live here. You're my son. My
grandson's father. When I go, it's all yours." Gahart
waved around at the darkness. "Hall, land, farmers,
herds, herders, servants, fighting men. Gold." He
gave the bag at his belt a little jingling shake.
"What say?"

Percival shook his head vigorously, like the red
charger when perplexed. Questions fairly flooded his
brain. He asked the first one that rose, fairly clear,
out of the flood. "When you go where, Lord?"

Gahart stared. Laughed. "To Hell, most like."

Hell. Alanna talked about Hell.

Ah. Goddamn! "When you die."

"Got it." Impatient, now. "Not even the greatest
Knight lives forever, you know. Enemy don't get
you, sickness will." (Percival felt Lili shudder at that
word, down beside him.) "Famine. Plain old age.
Gotta plan for that."

*Plan for that? Not me! I've got no plan for that now,
nor ever will!*

"So what say, friend? Interested?"

Lili touched Percival's knee. *She understands this, or
part of it. She'll tell me later.*

"This quest you mentioned."

"Oh, aye, that's not much! Just enough to prove
your worth."

"But what is it?"

"The Holy Grail."

???

"Never heard of the Holy Grail? Should have known!" It was Gahart's turn to shake his bemused head. "You just don't know nothing!"

"I come from a forest."

"Hmmmff. The Holy Grail is what Arthur's Knights quest after. I want it, myself."

"But what is it?"

"God's balls! It's a grail. A cup. A dish. Golden. Magic."

Some small thing in Percival's mind drew back, almost cautious. "Magic?"

"You say to it, 'Bring ale!' And right off, it's full of ale. Or meat. Or honeycake. Whatever you say that you can eat. Won't bring you gold."

Hmmm. Percival slipped his left hand down to meet Lili's hand. Her fingers clasped his and shook, *Yes!*

She doesn't mind it's magic? Neither do I.

One thing more. "You say Arthur's Knights quest for this grail. And you say Arthur will knight me. So—"

"I see your question. The grail won't do Arthur no good, Percival. He's better off without it."

"Why is that, Lord?"

"Arthur's Christian. Christian and magic, they don't mix. This grail would bring Arthur nothing but trouble. So a true Arthur's Man will grab it and hide it away before Arthur gets to it."

"Hah." *Lili will explain.*

"One reason I want it myself. Do Arthur a true service."

It's all falling into my hands!

Joy broke like light upon Percival's puzzled heart. *Never thought it would be so easy!*

"I think I will take up your quest!"

"You think so? I need more than think!"

"What do you need?"

Gahart felt in the bags and pouches on his belt. He brought out a medallion, a brooch, a small wooden animal figure, and dropped them all back in. "Cross'll have to do." He whipped a long knife out of a fold of robe, and thrust its hilt at Percival. "Take a hold on that."

Wondering, Percival took the hilt in his hand.

"Look, this is the Cross of Christ. Agreed?"

Percival felt the crosspiece on the hilt. Hilt and crosspiece did seem to form a cross. "Goddamn. Agreed." *At last, something I've heard of!*

"Say, 'On this Cross of Christ I swear I will quest for the Holy Grail.' Say that."

Percival said that.

"Say, 'I will not keep the grail myself. I will not take it to Arthur.' "

More hesitantly, Percival said that.

"Say, 'I swear on the Cross of Christ, if I find the Holy Grail, I will bring it back to good Lord Gahart.' "

Percival hesitated. Lili leaned reassuringly against his leg, and he said the words.

"Good. So be it." Gahart took the hilt-cross back in his own hand. "My turn. I swear on this Cross of Christ that when Percival brings me the Holy Grail

I will give him my daughter Ranna, and all the wealth that comes with her when I die. On my Knight's Honor."

He thrust the knife back out of sight in his robe. Yawned. Stretched. Stood up. "To bed, Percival. Tomorrow starts your training."

"Holy Michael Archangel! I'll have to *lie with her*?"

"That's what a husband does." This much I know. "You'll have to wed her. And that means bedding, and looking after, and staying with for always. Percival, this is what Human life is—one burden after another. Why under sky did you want to be Human?"

Miserably, "Because, goddamn, I am Human!"

We whisper and finger-talk by lamplight.

A stairway leads up from the hall to a narrow passageway giving onto three rooms above. The third room back, away from the stairs, is little Ranna's. She lives there with her old nurse. There they spin and weave most of every day. I don't know how Ranna can endure it, young and lively as she is. But I don't need the answer to that puzzle.

In the middle room, closer to the stairs, Lord Gahart sleeps in lonely luxury.

Percival and I sleep in this room, closest to the stairs. I would have had to sleep down in the hall with all the men, but I made Percival insist that I stay with him. I told him to say, "I need my servant Lil at all times."

Lord Gahart turned his smoldering little eyes on

me, and grunted. "Hah! So you're one of those," he said to Percival. "Very well. Let him stay."

So we're here together, whispering as the lamp sputters low. Around and below us the hall sinks into sleep and dream.

"That's how it will be," I tell Percival. "If you want to lord it in this hall, over what did he say—lands and herds and men and gold—you'll have to wed and be a husband. And a father."

"*Father?*"

"That's what Gahart said. Father of his grandson. And Percival, I won't be here to help you. Gods! I want to go home now!"

Grief grips my innards. I would give almost anything to walk again among close, sheltering trees, to lie half in a stream and tickle a trout, to listen to my own thought, and Spirit counsels brought by breezes.

This Kingdom is a cold, rough place!

I've wanted to go home since Percival led me—all unwilling—through a gate into walled Arthur's Dun.

There the jabbering Human crowd, the noise and stink and barren buildings overwhelmed me. I forget much of what happened there. I saw Niviene, and thought, *a friend*! I saw Percival stride up to the Red Knight and kill him; and I saw the faces of Arthur's Knights, angry, dangerous. Thank all Gods they were unarmed!

Then we were on the red horse, running away faster than I fly in dreams. At least we were out of the paved and walled space, thumping over fields.

But Percival, who should have guided and commanded the horse, had no notion how to do that. We would have lost him the first time we stopped and slid off, but that I sang a spell to bind him to us. All the following days I spent weaving spells about that horse; without magic, we could not get on him, stay on him, or catch him, (even hobbled.) I knew we should take off the bridle and saddle; but we knew not how, or how we would put them back on. So he wore them the whole time, although I felt pain each time I came near him.

He also thinned down fast, and finally went lame. When he staggered in here, the stable men clucked tongues and shook heads.

Magicking all day every day tired me out. I'm glad that now Percival is learning how to manage him the Human way, with spur and curb and whip.

Every day, besides, I had to reconvince Percival not to turn back to Arthur's Dun and ask King Arthur to knight him. He had not seen the furious faces of those Knights, as I had.

I think I managed all this only by grace of the Lady's Victory ring. She swung on her thong between my breasts every moment, strengthening, comforting. (I touch her now.)

Every day of our journey we saw astonishing things.

The most astonishing happened just before the horse started to limp. (And I had to sing a spell, lift his left hind foot, and find out why.)

We camped in a wood outside a village.

By then even Percival knew better than to enter

the village. Even he had noticed that villagers were curious about our clothes, his armor, and the red horse. Even he had noticed the eye-flash that meant, *we could kill these strangers, steal that horse!* So we camped outside in the wood.

But at dusk, wrapped in my invisible cloak, I sneaked in among the thatched huts and houses to see what I could steal. (Maybe a chicken; or Percival's favorite honeycakes! Or maybe another coverlet, now the horse could carry things.)

The place was quiet. Almost silent.

Humans are rarely that quiet, never silent.

My scalp prickled. Spine tingled. Something stank.

At the side of a house I poised on tiptoe—sniffing, listening—and heard, behind me, a delicate, silver tinkle.

I drew my "invisible" cloak close and shrank up small and still.

Firm, soft footfalls came toward my back. Two Humans approached behind me. I could not turn my head to look, and stay invisible; so I stood stiff and small, like a bush. My right hand found Bee Sting in my belt.

Lanternlight came about me.

The Humans stopped beside me; a boy, who carried a tinkling bell in one hand, and a lantern in the other; and a white-hooded man, who bore a small box in both hands like a treasure.

They saw me. The man turned toward me. I could not see his face under the white hood, but I felt his gentle gaze. Not to fear. His aura shone white and wide in the dark grey dusk, far brighter than the boy's lantern. Not to fear.

Kindly, he said to me, "Child, this is an un-good place for you to be."

I told him, "I know that, Sir. But I know not why."

And he told me, "There is sickness here."

Sickness! Oh Holy Goddess, *sickness* was what smelled so awful! I had smelled sickness before and fled from it, but nothing so bad as this.

He pointed to the house beside us. "In this house is plague. I must go in there. But you, child, go fast and far away from here, before you catch plague."

He meant, before plague caught me.

They went on then past me to the house corner. There the boy stopped and waited. The man took the lantern and went around the corner, I suppose into the plague house, as he had said.

I ran all the way back to camp. Tired as we were, we moved on that night.

I have wondered about that man ever since.

Why in the name of all Gods and fairies did he go into that house? Into that stink and danger? *Why did he pursue the plague?*

But so many strange things happened on this journey, I grew tired of questioning. I learned to accept whatever I saw, simply, as one does in dreams.

Now, Gods, I am tired!

Gahart's Hall is worse than Arthur's Dun.

Grieving or greedy ghosts drift here by night; Human souls still seeking their lost life.

By day evil-smelling giants stride about, roaring.

Lord Gahart swaggers in his large, muddy aura, shouting commands. And servants, invisible in their drab outfits as I in my cloak, rush to obey.

Gahart likes Percival.

When first we entered the courtyard, leading our lame red horse, the men would have taken horse and armor and thrust us outside. (I've made this out; something about our garments rouses contempt in even the poorest, saddest Humans.)

But Gahart looked at Percival. Those smoky eyes of his are sharper than they seem! As I see an aura, so Gahart saw the hidden Knight in Percival. At a glance, he looked past the garments and saw all the things he values most in men. I think in that glance he saw that Percival could find him this Holy Grail thing, and that Percival could father him a fine grandson, and that he could leave himself—the possessions which are himself—to no better heir.

And by his Human rules and understandings, he saw rightly. Percival is a goddamn good bet! Strong, big even by Human standards, Percival is made of ice. He feels no fear or doubt. Did he not kill the Red Knight without a moment's hesitation? He who before had only killed for meat! I had told him Merlin's stories by then; he knew that Knights killed Humans every day without a thought. And so he did, himself! He does simply, instantly, whatever he thinks Knights do. If Gahart asked him to hunt down a fire-breathing dragon, off he would go in a breath to hunt it down. I suppose he will lie with little Ranna in that same spirit, when the time comes.

Now he stares at me by lamplight. What did I say that keeps his exhausted blue eyes fixed on me?

"Lili! You won't go home till we find this Holy Grail!"

Ah. Aha. I said I want to go home.

Percival wants me to help him find this Holy Grail. How under sky can we find a magic cup? It sits on a shelf in a cupboard. It jounces in a horse's saddle-bag. It lies in a streambed, filling up with silt, somewhere in this Kingdom. And we don't even know the size of this Kingdom.

But I am here on my own quest.

A price is paid for every quest.
Draw heart's blood from out bared breast . . .

The price of my Human heart is high, so far. But not yet too high.

Gladly would I sneak out of here tonight and start the long, long walk home! (East, I know, and south. And I remember landmarks: a mill, a hall, a pasture full of great, glossy mares and frolicking foals.)

"I'm not going home tomorrow."

"You'll help me find the grail."

"I'll help you try."

Percival smiles and lies down. I draw our coverlet and his cloak up over him to his golden beard. His eyes sink shut, then pop open.

"Lili. Why did you not tell me that was Niviene, back there at Arthur's Dun?"

"I thought you knew." *Why wouldn't you know?*

"I don't know all the things you know."

Percival sighs, and sleeps.

No. You don't. If I held the Bird of Knowledge in my hands, you would hold one tail feather in yours.

Percival! What would you ever do without me?

I sit by his feet on the pallet, listening to the night. Owls hoot, patrolling the garden outside. Rats scurry, tiny nails clicking on wood or stone floors. Men snore down below in the hall. Gahart snores next door like thunder. Up on the roof, men walk and talk in low voices. Sentries. If you live in a visible, unmovable place like a hall, you have to guard it from enemies all night, every night.

About to blow out the lamp, curl down by Percival and draw my cloak over me, I pause.

Another night sound.

I've heard it before, other nights.

A creak; the *whsssh!* of a gown. Footsteps so soft, I'll bet the owl sailing past the arrow-slit windows doesn't hear them.

Little Ranna walks at night.

I call her "little" for her little, squashed soul. I see more of that than of her blooming body. She is taller than me, maybe older. And if you like curling, sunny hair (like Percival's!) and blue eyes, she is goddamn good-looking. But her aura is the width of a silk ribbon, all green and orange, and all twined around her pelvis. She hasn't a thought behind those blue eyes, or a Human Heart in her breast. It hasn't grown yet.

Maybe, it never will. I am beginning to suspect that not all Humans grow Hearts.

Other nights she has passed our door and gone on, softer than a mouse. I've been asleep before she ever returned.

But this night she stops outside our door.

And suddenly I know what she does at night.

That pelvic ribbon of aura should have told me that. I'm ashamed to be surprised.

And I know what's happened here. Little Ranna watched Percival break that dolt's jaw tonight, just as I did. (But from where? She must have a secret window into the hall. She's never seen in the hall with the men.)

And she thought the same thing I did. Except, because of my quest, I can't do it. And Percival's not ready for it, anyhow.

Little Ranna has no quest. And of course, she does not know that Percival is made of ice. No one would guess that.

In a flash I'm at the door. As it glides very carefully open, I'm in the doorway.

So is Ranna.

Each of us gives a little mousy jump at sight of the other. Ranna expected an empty doorway. I expected Ranna in her white, linen sleeping gown.

Robed in red-embroidered blue, fair hair curling over and down her shoulders, Ranna reminds me of a Human-story fairy. A wonderful scent of rose and lavender floats around her. Maybe this vision could even break Percival's ice!

"Lil!" She whispers.

I raise my hands to finger-talk. Then I remember, for all her beauty, poor Ranna is but Human. Doesn't understand finger-talk.

I whisper, "Outside."

With no demur at all, she turns and leads me into the dark passage. By the stair she draws back an ancient tapestry, so worn it has no color even by daylight, and reveals her secret window onto the hall below. A great wind of snores and body heat rises through the window, and utter darkness. Not even my Fey eyes can see down there now.

I wonder how Ranna, with only Human eyes, can wander here without a candle. She must know every half step of this hall by heart.

Beside the window, a second stairway leads away down. Ranna reaches back and takes my hand to guide me down through blackness.

Stair by stair she leads me carefully, not guessing that the very brightness of her unbound hair lights my way.

She does not notice the ghost that hovers before her, sinking stair by stair as she descends. I've seen this ghost before, always near Ranna—a young woman gowned like a servant. Her pale braid swings hip-length. She holds out strong-muscled arms as if to catch Ranna, should she stumble on the stair. At the bottom, she disappears.

Ranna pushes open a little, low door seemingly made for Fey. She crawls out through it. I follow, crouching. Here is the walled kitchen garden within the courtyard, spiderwebbed in silver dew. A low half-moon shines.

Ranna draws me into bushes against the wall. We kneel down. The guards on the roof won't see us here, even if they glance down. Ranna does everything easily, in a practiced way, as though many times before. With the same practiced ease she draws off her blue red-embroidered gown, I suppose to save it from the dewy grass. Rose-lavender scent bursts around her like dandelion seed. Bare-naked, moonwhite, slender, she turns to me. And opens her arms.

Ranna thinks I am a boy.

Whisper. "Gods! You're quick, Ranna!"

"Why not?"

"You do this every night?"

Shrug. "Only thing fun in life, you know?"

"I suppose weaving and spinning . . ."

Ranna spits, like her father, to the side. "I live for this. Worth the danger."

"Danger?" My ears perk up.

"Well, you know. If my father found out . . ."

"He doesn't know?" *How can he not?*

"God's balls, Lil! *Of course* he doesn't know! Why, if he knew . . ."

"What would he do?" This looks to be the most interesting night of our whole quest so far!

I repeat. "What would he do?"

Goddess! Poor little Ranna weeps. Tears flood her moonlit eyes and spill down her white-rose cheeks.

"Why under sky? What's it to him?"

"Lil, you're as strange as your master!"

Master? Oh. Percival. "Yes, well, we're foreigners here. Where we come from things are different."

"Where's that? Where is anything different?" I sense desperation in the question. Ranna wipes her eyes dry with leaves off our bush.

"We come from a forest far from here." Percival has already let that much out to Gahart. "Look, we haven't much time. Tell me why your father would care that you—"

"Why, how could he bear the insult!"

"Insult?"

"Or the loss! I would be no good to him!"

No good to him.

All at once, a mystery solves itself for me.

I see that Humans are all good for something to each other. Master and servant, husband and wife, peasants and lord, are all useful, each to each, one way or another. Their use binds them together. And this binding/bonding is their Survival Trick. Such bumbling, helpless creatures could no more survive alone than bees or ants could. Like this, each one learns a trick or two—how to fight, or how to spin, or how to grow peas—and they exchange their gifts and skills, and so they live.

Of what use to each other are father and daughter?

"What good are you?"

Ranna opens her mouth wide, baring little, shell-like teeth. She throws back her hand and gasps in a huge breath, and I know she means to laugh.

I leap and clap both hands over her mouth. The

sound that escapes, a rat might make. No sentry will look down the wall for that noise.

Laughing, Ranna falls backward under the bushes. I crawl on top of her, holding the sound down. Here, I learn something I never knew before, that laughter can catch you like sickness. Before Ranna sobers I am half-laughing, myself.

We lie still entwined, like lovers. I whisper, "But surely, Ranna, the men must talk among themselves about . . ."

"Wouldn't dare! Never dare! They'd be hanged . . . used for arrow practice . . . fed to the hounds."

Holy blessed Gods! A good thing I warned Percival to stay clear of this girl! I noticed the men did, so it seemed the wise course to follow. But I never guessed the matter was so serious!

"Will this happen to me if . . ."

"Be assured! But Lil, I thought you knew that. I would not have led you here . . ."

Goddamn! Seems a high price for a bit of fun! But . . . But . . . if it's such a secret . . . "What will you do if the Goddess blesses you, Ranna?"

"What?"

"How will you explain a newborn babe to your father?"

"Oh. No. Nurse is a midwife." Whatever that is. "And a witch."

Truly? I have seen no sign of that in the sleepy old woman's aura.

"She knows how to get rid of it. We did that once already."

What? "You did what?"

"Got rid of it. The babe. No one guessed anything."

I stare into Ranna's soft, wet eyes. I untangle and withdraw from her, put wet grassy earth between us. "You destroyed the Goddess's gift?" Which might have grown into a perfect child with no fingernail missing? And maybe as lovely as Ranna herself!

But then look again, with Human eyes. This child would have been no good at all to Ranna. I'm learning to think Human! *Oh, how wise I feel!*

"I got rid of it. Lil, stop talking! Or are you too scared now?"

Ranna reaches for me.

I scoot farther back away.

Ranna smiles wide-mouthed. "I know! It's your first time, isn't it! You don't know—"

"Ranna—"

"I'll show you how, Lil." Lovely white arms open wide. "I'll show you so you'll never forget! Or be satisfied with anyone else!"

"Ranna, I only came to tell you something." *And thank all Gods, you told me something!*

"What? You came here to *talk*?"

"Aye. To tell you about my . . . my master. Percival."

Her eyes light up like the moon.

"He's no good, Ranna. He's made of ice."

"Not that man!"

"Ah, yes. That man. He thinks of nothing but Knighthood. Chivalry."

Ranna shudders. "Uuuugh. Then he . . . he might tell my father!"

A good thought! "Indeed, he might! Think well on that, Ranna."

I roll away out of the thicket. I find my feet and vanish into the little Fey doorway before Ranna can blink, before a sentinel looking down from the roof can know what he saw, or if he saw anything.

Let little Ranna wonder, too!

Whisking up the black-dark stairs I wonder—*why did I warn Ranna off Percival?*

I'm glad I did. I've learned more tonight than on our whole quest so far.

White under first snow, meadows stretched to low, encircling hills. Surprised by snow, migrating ducks talked and dabbled in a narrow streambed hidden among reeds.

A hunting harrier dropped out of sunny air to skim above the reeds.

Percival paced his red charger along the reeds.

The red was sleek, now, well fed and furnished. Lili had learned well the care of him from Lord Gahart's stable men. And Gahart had taught Percival to handle him.

This Percival was new, armed in helmet and cuirass, lance at hand, unblazoned shield hooked to his saddle. Lord Gahart had armed and sent him forth to search for King Arthur, who was rumored to be traveling this way. For the new, proud, prepared Percival was still unknighted.

He noticed the harrier swoop on wide-stretched wings over the reeds. *Goddamn! Might maybe pick up a bite here!*

Back behind the western hill, Lili tended their campfire. She might have found them something to cook, by now; or she might not. Percival's stomach shrank and complained beneath its armor. At this hungry moment more scavenging Fey than proud Knight, Percival turned the red after the harrier.

Which dropped into reeds.

Ducks squawked, screamed and flapped up in thunderous flocks.

The harrier rose slowly, clutching a heavy brown teal in its talons.

Percival slapped gloved hand to where Bee Sting should lie against his hip. *Holy Hubert, I forgot! Knights don't carry Bee Stings!*

But all the same, the teal dropped in his path. The harrier dived right after it into the snow, grabbed it in a firmer grip and flapped away, showering snow.

Hungry Percival was left with a snow hole framed in teal feathers.

He reined in and looked down into the hole.

Pure, new snow formed a perfect grail; like the empty, golden one he had handed to the Queen in Arthur's Dun. But this grail brimmed with blood.

Percival dismounted. He stood looking into the snow grail. Vaguely he knew that the ducks had settled back into the reeds, that the sun had gone behind a cloud and then returned. He saw these things from the corner of his mental eye, while his true vision concentrated itself in the bloody snow grail at his feet.

Percival was little Percy, back in the Fey forest.

He stood with smaller Lili before the statue of Mary. Snow fell upon them, and through Mary's lattice roof, and upon Mary. Mary and Christ were mantled in snow, softer than ermine fur.

Alanna had given Percy a reed brush and sent him to clean off the statue.

As he raised the brush, Lili vanished from beside him. Ever, she was fearful of Mary . . .

The red charger nickered at Percival's shoulder.

Vaguely, he heard sounds of a horse approaching, the *clink!* of metal and *creak!* of harness. He gathered his wits and looked up.

There came a heavyset Knight toward him on a grey charger, armed as he was, lance at rest. Twenty feet away he stopped the grey and lifted his shield to show its identifying device—a red griffin couchant on a blue field. Loudly, formally, he said, "Sir Knight! Know you that King Arthur camps over yonder hill?" And pointed north.

Equally formal, Percival said, "Truly, Sir, I knew that not. As for me, I am camped over yonder hill." And he pointed west. With difficulty he held his attention on this, his first knightly encounter with an armed stranger. His mind yearned back to the snow grail.

The stranger said, "The King commands your presence at his hunting camp. He has sent me, Sir Cai, his

foster brother, to escort you there. You have heard of
me."

Sir Cai. Yes, Percival had heard of him. Now he
looked him up and down. *Big. Mostly fat. Stern. But
lazy. Look at those brown cow's eyes! This is not the man
who can take me from my meditation.*

In rudely plain language, Percival replied; "Sir, go
back to the King. Tell him I will come to him shortly.
I have a matter to attend here first."

He glanced down into the grail. The magic, vision-
ary blood was just beginning to seep away, turning
the snow rosy.

Sir Cai snorted like a horse. "You venture to command me, Sir? Like a herald, a messenger? Look you
to me, here!"

Straining, Percival drew his eyes and half his mind
back to Sir Cai.

Cai took his lance in hand and shook it. "Mount
and follow me, Sir. Or I drive you to the King at the
point of this lance."

Percival sighed. Not so easily would he be rid of
Sir Cow Eyes. "You challenge me, Sir?"

Snort! "You know who I am. I know you not. Yet
I honor you with my challenge. Aye! Mount and
meet me."

Sir Cai turned his grey and trotted far enough back
to give space for a charge. There he faced Percival
again and couched his lance.

Scenting action at last, the sleek, eager red nodded,
blew and pawed snow as Percival mounted.

He settled himself firmly, couched lance, raised

shield. Across the snowy space Sir Cai's raised shield bloomed like a huge flower.

Lo. The grey charger started forward, great hooves tossing snow.

The red needed no nudge. It burst into an eager trot. Ears perked forward, it moved into a canter.

This was Percival's first true challenge. Often enough he had charged a dummy, or a friendly teacher. But now the thought touched his mind, *Cow Eyes means to run that lance through me. Hah! Goddamn!*

Forward like thunder.

Under Sir Cai's helmet his ferocious grin came clear and close.

Gahart murmured in Percival's head, *Don't look at his face. Look at his shield.*

Percival tilted his lance straight at the griffin.

Look to his point. Shift shield against it. Now, shift aim.

The horses charged together.

Percival's lance struck home. The impact knocked him back in his saddle. As the horses cantered past each other, precise as dancers, he swayed, caught the saddle horn, found his balance.

With no urging the red slowed and half circled and stopped.

Back there the grey waited quietly beside its master, who lay spread-eagled on the snow.

Percival trotted back, dismounted, and drew his bright new sword.

Should Another challenge you,
Seize sword or lance and run him through.

"Hey!" Sir Cai's brown cow eyes popped open. He held up a warding hand. "I yield! Hold off!"

Hampered by his heavy cuirass, he sat up and said in the low language of every day, "Have it your way. I'll go tell the King you'll come later."

He's surprised. He didn't expect me to kill him.

Gahart murmured in Percival's head, *Go easier. Good men don't grow in gardens.*

Hah. Aye. This is one of Arthur's good men. And a foster brother besides.

Percival sheathed his sword and stood back. "Very well. Take you my message to the King."

Urgently, the snow grail called to him. He turned toward it, then back. *See Cow Eyes off, first. This one might rise up and strike from behind.*

With difficulty, Sir Cai heaved himself up, brushed off snow and mounted his grey. With no farewell, he rode past Percival and away north, along his own trail. His broken lance lay forgotten in the snow.

Instantly, Percival strode to his snow grail. The red ambled behind, blowing warm breath down his neck.

Thick, warm blood still half filled the snow grail.

Percival's mind sank into it, as a man sinks into a bog.

The Fey forest again, again under snow. Young Percy, almost grown, came upon two Fey boys dressing a young pig in a snowbank.

For a change, he saw them before they saw him, because they were deeply intent upon their work. He also saw, smelled and heard three wolves slinking through thickets toward the blood.

Without thought, he moved to help the boys.

Poisoned darts found the two closest wolves. The third whirled and bounded away. And now the Fey boys looked up.

His interference surprised them. They themselves would have passed on and let the hunters fight off their own wolves.

But they were generous with their pig meat, if not with their friendship.

Percival sighed.

Nearby, the red muttered. It had moved off to graze through snow; now it stood alert, ears pricked, looking north. And now Percival heard the *creak!* and *clang!* of another horse and rider.

He turned north to see a tall, black-plumed Knight atop a great black stallion raise his shield in greeting. The shield was white, crossed by three red bands.

Argent, three bends gules! Goddamn, goddamn! Gahart said.

The Knight reined in his black, and said, loudly courteous, "Sir Knight, King Arthur requires your presence now at his hunting camp. I, Sir Lancelot, will escort you."

Percival examined Sir Lancelot, Arthur's Best Knight. He liked the man's seat on his horse. He liked his manner, and open, almost friendly face. *A joust with Lancelot will test my best powers! Gahart said he is not allowed to joust because he cannot be overthrown.*

Sir Lancelot said into Percival's silence, "Sir, of your courtesy, mount and ride with me now. Unless you wish to fight for your right to stand here and contemplate snow."

Percival bowed his head to Sir Lancelot. Wordless, he went and mounted the red charger.

Sir Lancelot flashed a signal with his shield, turned, rode away and turned back.

Percival settled himself firmly and couched his lance. *Saint George, give me victory now!*

Lo, the black charger trotted forward, great hooves tossing snow. Lancelot leaned low and forward. Sharp sun glinted off the oncoming point of his lance.

The black reached a canter.

So did the red. Percival had moved into combat without full realization. Already he was halfway to a clash with Arthur's Best Knight.

Arthur will have no better Knight than . . .

Unknown, unguessed strength flooded Percival.

Look at his point. It aims low. He will strike high. Raise shield. Lower lance.

CRASH.

The impact lifted Percival wholly clear of his saddle.

With a stupendous *crack!* His lance broke and flew away in two parts.

He felt himself struck, low.

Heavy armor not withstanding, he flew up in air.

He grabbed the saddle horn, swayed, found balance. The red slowed, half circled, and stopped.

Lance broke. We finish with swords. Hah! Goddamn!

Lancelot lay on his back in snow, under his broken lance.

Good men don't grow . . . Pray Heaven he is not hurt!

Snorting and prancing, the red trotted Percival back to Lancelot. *Holy Hubert! There was anger enough when I killed the Red Knight . . . If I have harmed Arthur's Best Knight—*

Percival slung shield on saddle and dismounted.

Lancelot's grey eyes looked up, conscious.

He sat up. Shook his head. Gazed wonderingly at Percival.

Percival reached and grasped his hand. Slowly, he hauled large, armed Lancelot to his feet. Panting, they stood together. Percival's helmet still rang from the encounter.

But even now the snow grail called to him, louder than battle-echo.

Lancelot asked, "What message shall I take to the King?"

"That I . . . will come to him shortly."

"And who shall I say sends him this message?"

"I am . . . Sir Percival."

Lancelot nodded, took off his helmet and straightened its plume.

Fearing no treachery this time, Percival strode away to his snow grail.

Blood stood much lower in the grail.

In the few remaining drops shone the sky.

Percival stood in full, open sunlight on the North River Cliffs and stared up in the blue sky-depths. Deeper and deeper he stared, swaying where he stood. His soul soared, then drifted, higher and higher into blind blue. Silently, his soul called, *"Here am I! Where are You?"*

Silence answered from Silence.

Green snow fell and hid the sky.

A spell broke.

Percival awoke.

He was looking into a young, handsome face—dark beard, grey, good-humored eyes.

The unknown Knight had cast his green cloak down over the snow grail. It lay there still, soaking up the last magic blood.

He said, "Sir Percival, you have been enchanted."

"Goddamn! That must be so . . ."

"That is why you twice refused to come to King Arthur at his command."

"I did? . . ."

The Knight smiled. "Are you spell-free now?"

Percival drew a deep breath and looked about him.

Here he stood with this strange Knight in a snowy meadow beside a stream. Ducks gabbled in reeds. Geese flew, calling, from the low northern hills to the southern.

Behind the western hill he would find his own camp. Maybe Lili was cooking, there. *Starving!*

And behind the northern hill, he had been told, King Arthur rested in a hunting camp.

"Aye . . . Now I remember myself . . . and who came to me earlier . . . and I told them I would go to the King later because . . . because . . ."

"Something under here enchanted you." The Knight pulled his green cloak up out of snow. "Better you not look again. I'll tell you what is here . . . Nothing. A little bloody snow hole, with feathers. Looks like a harrier struck here."

"Aye. A harrier struck. Yet it seemed . . ."

The Knight swirled his stained cloak up about him and pinned it. "Sir Percival, let us ride to the King. I who invite you am Sir Gawain."

Another known name! "Sir Gawain, I come."

But before mounting his charger, Percival bent and plucked up a bloody teal feather from snow. He poked it into his pouch.

Riding north beside Sir Gawain, he said "I have been seeking the King. To ask him to make me a Knight."

Sir Gawain turned an astonished face to him. "Sir! You are no Knight?"

"I am not yet knighted."

"Ech! Holy Michael! God Himself must have knighted you, Sir Percival." And Gawain muttered to himself, "What will Lancelot say to this!"

At the top of the hill they drew rein.

Arthur's hunting camp spread away below. Hobbled horses, hounds running loose, huntsmen and unarmed Knights mingled among blue and red tents. Pennants flapped in a rising breeze.

And in the midst, over the largest, snow-white tent, Arthur's golden dragon swung in the wind.

GAHART'S COUNSEL

I'll waste no word. No bard am I.
Righter than Roman road must lie
The trail we travel till we die;
The Knights' Road.

Meet you a maiden passing fair?
No husband, father, guardian there?
She is your prize, your jewel rare,
On the Knights' Road.

To church with others wend your way
To bend and bow, to plead and pray.
But to your sword true worship pay
On the Knights' Road.

Upon your way you hear a cry?
Rush to respond! There's riches nigh.
Gold or girl will satisfy,
On the Knights' Road.

Victor, slaver not to slay.
You'll have debts enough to pay
Should you ever lose the day,
On the Knights' Road.

Follow faithfully your King,
For in his gift lies everything
That war may win or bards may sing,
On the Knights' Road.

Beneath your breastplate beats a heart
That laughs and longs and breaks apart
Withered, withdrawn. Walk, by this art,
The Knights' Road.

4

Lost Knight

On the highest cliff over North River Alanna stood against a biting wind.

Far below, North River roared around ice-capped rocks. Ahead, the end of sunset streaked a grey, winter sky. Around and behind, firming ice sheathed the cliffs.

Within, as always, was Percy.

I sent him forth with a soup-kettle helmet, three-colored clothes and a headful of half-truths, a fool among thieves. I hoped the folk out there would take him for a God-touched madman and leave him alone.

And I thought he would learn that his truly crazed dream of being knighted was impossible.

And then . . . he would come home.

But here it is, half a year, and my Percy is not back.

Either he is dead; or he is a Knight.

So Percy is dead. My son is dead. Never coming home.

For days, Alanna had been thinking of ways to die. *Holy Mary, how I long for it! To fly free of this bone-aching, heart-broke body! No tears in Heaven.*

Ivie must be in Heaven. How good to see my Ivie again! I never dreamed how I would miss her, till she went.

Sir Ogden is there, surely. Not by his fault, he raised his sons the only way he knew.

And my boys! Kimball and Locke, Owen and Oak, Chad and Brand, Powell and Olin!

And my Percy. If not now, then surely soon.

But Alanna could not simply hurl herself off the Cliffs like a sick old Fey. That was against God's Law. Taking her own life she would find herself in Hell. *Never see a loved face again! No love in Hell.*

Dear God. (As she still called the Fey "Good Folk," Alanna called God "Dear," hoping that the Creator of childbirth, sickness, death, human nature and winter might be won over by blandishments.) *Dear God, now it is in Your hands.*

So she had come here to the highest Cliff and walked out to the edge, across thin, crackling ice, to watch the winter sun set. Here, wind could topple her. She could fall on ice and whisk down over the edge in a breath. Turning to walk back, she could slip. Or, God could guide her feet safely back from the edge. Did He want her here in this Vale of Tears? The choice was His.

Not my will, but Thine, be done. Aye. Amen.

Lower sank sun over forest.

Time to go home, if I'm going. The trails must be almost dark now, back under the trees.

Heart within spoke. *Lo! Percy is alive! If not, I would have told you.*

And were Percy still alive, there was still a chance . . . a small chance . . . that he might come home.

*He might. And in that case, maybe . . . right now . . .
I don't want to die. Yet.*

Time to go home.

Carefully, Alanna turned her back to wind and
sunset. *Holy Mary! This ice firmed up while I stood here!*

Glare ice shone sunset-rose for twelve, fourteen
steps across sloping rock.

Glancing around for a foothold, Alanna caught
movement in the corner of an eye.

Some God-forsaken Fey spying the way they do—

He stepped out into last light and stretched a hand
toward her.

—Sir Edik! Kind, dear Sir Edik!

He caught hold of a birch and leaned as far forward as he could. Alanna leaned and stretched. But
their reaching fingers grasped cold, empty wind.

"Sir Edik!" Alanna's cry was lost, wind-carried,
drowned in North River's roar.

He raised his hands and finger-talked.

"Slower! Talk slower!"

He paused; nodded; began again. *Stay. There. Wait.*

"Aye! I'll wait!" Vigorously, she nodded.

Dear Sir Edik vanished, Fey-like, into dark woods.

Alanna stood, frozen against the bitter wind that
pushed at her back and billowed her cloak like a sail.

He reappeared, dragging a long, crotched pine branch.
He hooked the crotch around the birch and pushed the
branching, needled end across the ice to Alanna.

If her frozen hands could grasp it . . . She gasped
in a breath of wind, leaned, and grabbed for the
pine needles.

They tore out in her hands.

Tottering, she grabbed the slender pine tips beneath. Holding on with all her strength, she took two steps up and forward. Her feet slithered on ice. She fell.

Ice burned through the length of her new wool gown that the Lady's own hands had carded, spun, woven and sewn. North River echoed between her ears. She felt her feet swing out and down and over the edge. Freezing wind bit her ankles.

With numb hands she gripped the pine tips.

To Heaven with Percy!

Not yet. Not now.

Alanna began pulling herself up the branch.

And the branch itself dragged her, inch by inch, up the ice.

Must hold on . . .

Fingers touched hers.

Dear Sir Edik, feet hooked around his birch, had dragged her so far up that he could reach her hand.

At the end of her strength, she let go the branch and caught his hand. Only after, creeping up the ice between his hand and the branch, did she realize what she had done.

Could have gone over in that instant!

Snow burned over her shoulder, under her breast. *That's snow. Not ice.*

Snow under her hips. *Pull. Hang on. Creep.*

Her feet sank into snow.

I'm off the ice. I'm up here with dear Sir Edik.

He caught her in his arms. Hers clasped his neck tight. Together, they rolled like youngsters in soft snow.

SIR EDIK'S COUNSEL

Snow and pine boughs knit a nest;
Hidden heart in icy breast.
Hidden, let's perch wing to wing;
Perch and preen and nearly sing
Canticles to hidden Spring.

5

Knight of the Round Table

"Can this be Lili?"

Softly, I laugh for joy.

Niviene knows me most certainly by sight and aura and smell and Spirit. But little Ranna's blue, red-embroidered gown surprises her!

I hardly know myself, gliding about Arthur's Dun in this finery, black hair combed loose down my back! I have never worn anything like this gown. At first it needed some practice. I had to learn to kick the (shortened) skirt away with each step; or else to lift it gracefully up and away. I remembered Percival, learning to walk in armor, with some sympathy.

But I learned also a new joy—a power of attraction and excitement; the exact opposite of invisibility. And the glances of passing men and boys confirmed this power. Anywhere else in the Kingdom this would signal acute danger. But here in Arthur's Dun Human men live strictly constrained and governed, at least in daylight. These men's glances sent me only appreciation and added power; the men themselves passed on quietly.

In any case, I still wear my Bee Sting; and Victory still hides between my breasts.

So defended, I have wandered by night to Niviene's fireside in the mages' hut.

Niviene gestures me to fold myself down beside her. She sits by her hearth coals in a rosy cloud of ember light and white aura. Gracious, she offers me bread and mutton. "Where did you steal that gown?"

I tell her about little Ranna.

"You favored her, stealing it! She plays a dangerous game."

"She knows that. And she has other gowns."

"Sorrow for her! Now, our Percy; we see him doing very well!"

"He's in the chapel this moment."

"Keeping his vigil for Knighthood."

"I like not the chapel." *So I came here, to you.*

Niviene chuckles. "No more do I! The Power there . . . will you have ale, Lili?"

"Water." Niviene needs not to get up; she only reaches into shadow and brings forth full goblets. "You knew I was coming!"

"We thought you might. So, Lili, what do you think of the Kingdom?"

This is too much to tell!

I begin slowly, sipping water between thoughts. "I could say I hate the Kingdom . . . All that dirt." Niviene nods. "Fury . . . Gods, so much noise! No Human, no animal, doing their own will." Niviene nods deeper. "All like . . . worker bees. Even Spirits seem drawn into Human frenzy."

"What Spirits?"

Why does Niviene ask that? Surely, she sees them too. "Mostly ghosts; some dead, some yet alive, Alanna comes around Percy . . . Percival, he wants to be called . . . morning and night."

"Most like, when she prays for him."

"Mother ghosts, live and dead, hover near their small children. Dead ghosts drift about every hut and street. I meet very few fairies."

"The massive Human aura is too strong for them."

"Sometimes Gods appear, beating wings like windy clouds."

"Angels. Take care with angels. Not all of them are kind."

"They guard Arthur's chapel. And I saw one in a Human hut, where they gave us their bed and most of their dinner."

Niviene finger-talks, *That would draw an angel.*

"But all these spirits seem concerned with Human doings. No more free than the Humans themselves."

Why did you come out here, Lili?

I crumble bread, lick crumbs off my fingers. Sip water.

"I came here to find a Human Heart."

Niviene laughs.

"Truly. Merlin told me the Human Heart is the World's Greatest Magical Power."

"Even so, I would not go searching for it! Any more than I would walk into a plague-haunted house! I threw away my own, Fey heart, long ago."

That reminds me. "Niviene, the Lady counseled me to chastity."

Good counsel. Though she does not herself follow it.

"Are you chaste, Niviene?"

I am.

"But . . . what of the Goddess, and Her sacrifice?"

Does pain flit across Niviene's cold face?

Nay! That must have been a trick of firelight.

Calmly she signs, *I sacrificed once to the Goddess. Once was enough. She can demand no more of me. As for you, you have time enough for that.*

Think about this later. "And has this chastity strengthened your Power?"

Niviene raises and jabs both thumbs at the glowing coals on the hearth. On the instant, hungry flames leap high. Niviene continues to point. In the flame, Percival appears. "What do you think, little one?"

Fully armed, sword held upright before him in both hands, Percival kneels before the high altar in Arthur's chapel. In dark air above him Alanna's pale face, pale braid, shine softly.

"See, Niviene! Alanna is there."

Pointing, Niviene cannot finger-talk. "There; but not aware."

"She doesn't know she's there?"

"Most likely she dreams."

Ah. So even Humans travel in dreams!

We watch Percival nod, sway and jerk upright again.

"Holy Gods! Must he kneel there till dawn, like this?"

"His own choice, Lili."

"Not so! He must follow the rule!"

"His choice to follow the rule. His choice to be a Knight."

I sigh. "Poor Alanna! Tomorrow her long nightmare comes true. Percival truly becomes a true Knight."

A voice from the dark behind us says, "If she ever hears of this, Alanna may well leap off the Cliffs."

We turn toward the back of the hut. Merlin emerges from the dark.

Robed in white, crowned and cloaked by his huge white aura, he advances nimbly to hunker down between us.

"Hear that?" Niviene says to me. "Throw herself off the Cliffs! That's what a Human Heart will do for you!"

She lowers her pointing thumbs, and Percival fades from the fire. The flame sinks back down into coals.

"No question," says Merlin, reaching for bread. "The Human Heart is itself the price of its magic—a heavy burden to carry. As for the magic, the owner must know how to handle it." Bite, chew, swallow. "Fortunately for us, most Humans have no notion how to handle it. They let it handle them. Thus, such confusion reigns in their world that they must leave us alone!" Grin; wink.

Somewhat confused myself, I say, "I seek a Heart. But Percival seeks the Holy Grail."

"The Holy Grail?"

Merlin's gnarled fingers pause, breaking bread. Niviene's dark eyes darken.

Merlin asks me, "He is not content to attain Knighthood, itself? Now he wants the Holy Grail?"

I tell them about Lord Gahart, his daughter, lands, herds, men and so forth. "All this he will give Percival in return for the Holy Grail."

Niviene gasps. "But, Arthur! Percival's alliegance is to Arthur! How can he hand over the grail to this . . . Gahart?"

I explain. "Gahart says that Arthur is better off without the grail. As a Christian, he should rightly have no dealings with magic."

"Magic?" Merlin breaks his bread. "What magic?"

"Gahart says the grail is a magic dish that brings forth whatever food and drink is desired."

"Hah." Pop bread in mouth. Swallow hard. "The grail is the Cup of the Last Supper."

Last supper?

"Christ's last supper before His death on the cross."

Confusion floods!

"But," Merlin adds, chewing, "it matters not."

Matters not?

"No questing Knight will ever lay earthly eyes on the Holy Grail." And Merlin laughs.

Niviene and I bow respectful heads to this true laughing prophecy.

"As to your Percival . . ." Break the last bread; share it around. "Your Percival will never see the grail with any eyes at all, so long as he is made of ice.''

Percival woke, still upright; sword still upstanding between numb hands.

The sanctuary lamp glowing softly on the altar reflected on the golden door of the Tabernacle. Percival understood, now, that God lived behind that golden door. Earnestly, though foggily, he gazed at the door, and tried to send thoughts through it to God—Who seemed to sleep.

I come here from far away. I come from a Fey forest, where I knew nothing. Now, in this coming morning, King Arthur will knight me. I will become a Knight of the Round Table! I, Percival; I, who knew nothing! Lord, do You hear me?

The sanctuary lamp flickered in darkness.

Then, Lord, come spring, I will quest for the Holy Grail! I who have come so far will go farther. I will find the grail, and I will take it to Lord Gahart, who taught me much. You will be glad of that, Lord; for King Arthur, my liege Lord, should not deal with magic. It is not Your will that he should do so. Am I right?

The lamp dimmed. *Maybe the oil's low? Nay, not so. I am falling asleep.*

Lord, let me not sleep! This night I must meditate on my life to come, on adventures and virtues and heroisms . . .

When I take the grail to Lord Gahart, he will give me all that he has.

Not all at once. I will share it all with him while he lives. But Gahart is old, Lord. Soon he will go on to You in Heaven, and leave me his fields, his flocks and herds, his shepherds and plowmen . . .

Visions of Gahart's lands swam like dreams through Percival's mind. He saw raucous, violent men thoughtlessly obedient to him. He saw flagons and barrels of ale, constantly refilled; the very Holy Grail itself would belch honeycakes and fine, soft bread at a word from him! *No need to hunt my rich woodlands; roast grouse will fly up out of my grail!*

But I will hunt, if only to keep myself strong. And I will fight at the King's call, all days, all seasons. And King Arthur will have no finer Knight than me, Sir Percival. Glad he will be forever that he knighted me! Lord, do You hear this?

Behind the golden door, God slept.

Kneeling stiff and still as a wooden statue, Percival sent his thought like a battering ram at the golden door.

Lord God, You have ever slept when I sought you! I never found You in the forest, I have not found You in the Kingdom, and now I find You not in Your own golden Tabernacle! Lord God, I look at You! All my life I have looked at You, and never once have You looked back at me! Look back at me now! Look back at me now!

Again, Percival swayed and caught himself.

You sleep. But I must not.

Some say I am made of ice. You, God, are made of rock!

He let his drooping eyes roam the dark.

Over there . . . the Mary statue. Bigger than Alanna's. But the same.

Like Alanna's Mary, this one held one compassionate hand out to Her petitioner. Her Christ son rested on Her other, open hand. This Mary was also robed, crowned and haloed; and Her paint had not worn away under rain and snow, but still reflected golden lamplight.

Yet She's the same . . .

Dreamy Percival drifted near the statue in Mary's Clearing.

Below him, Alanna's snowy garden waited for distant spring. A humped, shapeless figure huddled before Mary. It seemed to hug itself, sway and weep; but Percival, though seeing clear as by daylight, could hear no sound.

A second figure moved below him. Old Sir Edik bent to the huddled form, hugged and patted and raised it.

It turned and embraced him, and raised unseeing eyes to Percival.

Percival thought, *Mother, never fear for me! King Arthur will have no better Knight. This has been prophesied with laughter.*

But lo, Mary's Clearing had vanished.

Percival knelt alone, stiff and numb, before the mild glow of sanctuary lamp and Tabernacle. Around him hung darkness.

Windy clouds chase winter sunshine across Arthur's Dun.

The mages and I are far from the only ones come to see Percival knighted!

Disguised as a short Human lady in Ranna's gown

and my "invisible" cloak, I must have begun to feel the part I acted; for I have let myself become part of a gathering, smelly Human crowd. Now here I stand in the middle of it, I who would rather peek like a mouse spy from roof or drain!

Along Percival's path from chapel door across to King's Hall door stand Round Table Knights— Gawain, Lancelot, Cai, Bors, Bedevire, Gareth, and more—their squires and servants behind them.

Except for Lancelot's small, brown squire, Mell, who grins and chats in Lancelot's ear.

Gwenevere waits by the great doors to King's Hall, with a small contingent of bright-robed ladies.

Servants, traders, beggars, slaves, wives and children block the street both ways, peering over shoulders and between cloaks, as I should do, myself. Somehow as the crowd gathered I lost myself in it. Now I stand in the front row across from Merlin and Niviene, perfectly visible from all sides, "invisible cloak" or no, and crowd-trapped.

I should be terrified but Victory dangles by my heart. And Ranna's magnificent gown disguises me. And of course, Bee String hangs by my hand.

This is a new art I learn here; if you cannot be a shadow, or a bush, be a respectable Human! There may be some safety in that.

Clouds chase sunshine across the Dun; when a dark cloud sweeps over, auras shine out. Quickly, I glance around.

Over there by King's Hall, Gwenevere's small, green aura clings close and bright. One strand reaches out and streams across wind, toward . . . Lancelot.

Lancelot's orange-green aura reaches toward Gwenevere; and the two auras meet and circle and converse, while all eyes are locked on the chapel door.

But . . . Gwenevere is, what's the word, *wed*, to Arthur. Not to Lancelot. *Think about this later.*

I pass on to Squire Mell. Something unusual about Mell . . . he is beardless, though certainly adult. His constant smile is close-mouthed, tight-lipped. His narrow, cautious aura like a soft rainbow . . .

Lancelot's Squire Mell is Fey!

He may be the Lady's lost son, Lugh!

Think about this later.

Side by side, Merlin and Niviene shine steadily, grandly, like two huge stars. But I remind myself, the Humans around them do not see them shine. Alone in the foremost crowd they sport no jewelry; no necklace, bracelet, earring, finger ring, buckle or brooch proclaims their worth. Only the stern message of their white robes and mistletoe crowns keeps the pressing crowd a little away.

Sun chases shade; auras fade.

The quietness of this crowd surprises me. Where I find Humans gathered I expect noise. But these folk are almost silent, eyes on the chapel door, faces . . . solemn. Looking up into these big, still faces, I almost feel thoughtful minds behind.

Aha! A murmur runs like a gentle stream down the street.

The chapel door opens.

Within is darkness; within the dark, a golden flame; within the flame, a Human figure.

The crowd sighs, admiring.

Can Humans see auras after all?

Maybe they can sense auras, as I sometimes sense deeply invisible Spirits.

Percival emerges from darkness into winter sunlight. Sunlight devours and quenches his golden flame. Tall he stands on the top chapel step; big and broad and bright—all the things we Fey laughed to scorn. These Humans murmur admiration.

Percival! You came to your right world!

Grave, radiant, he steps down into the path left open, and progresses—that's the world—toward King's Hall.

First Gawain, then Lancelot, moves to escort him. One on each side they lead him between the mages and me, past Gwenevere, to the King.

For while we all watched Percival, King Arthur has appeared on the top step of King's Hall.

Big and dark, bright-bejewled, he awaits Percival, sword naked in his two gloved hands.

Naked sword? Why does the King need a sword?

Sudden dread shivers up and down my spine.

Nothing is so strange that Humans will not do it.

Maybe at this ceremony the King decides whether Percival is worthy to be a Knight; then, depending on his decision, he either knights him, or slays him on the spot.

I haul Victory by her thong up out of my gown.

As I have done before, I point her at Percival's back, pouring Power into Percival.

Nay! If there were real danger, the crowd would emanate excitement. And the only excitement I feel here is reverent joy.

And my Percival can well defend himself, even without Bee Sting, which he has so foolishly laid aside.

Pouring Power on Percival between concealing fingers, I look again at Arthur.

In glowing, growing sunlight, King Arthur's triple aura shines red as new-shed blood closest to his rugged form; farther out shimmers a wide orange band; and farther yet—higher, wider than the doors of King's Hall—a faint gold band twinkles like sunlit water.

I have seen the King's aura before; but not magnified and solemnized by ritual, nor enriched by the crowd's pooled Power; as now I see it.

Holy Gods! I drop Victory back down inside my gown. Not even Victory can defend against such Power.

Who ever guessed a Human could shine like that?

Close, closer, to the King.

Arthur stood on the top step of the King's Hall door, sword in hands, watching Percival's approach.

Goddamn! My hour is come!

Percival had always believed it would. It had to come, this hour of triumph, vindication and final acceptance. From his forest meeting with Sirs Friendly,

Suspicious, and Wounded, he had never for a moment doubted that this was his appointed fate.

But now, as the crowd stood aside for him; now, as his friends came beside and escorted him; now, as the King awaited him, he marveled. *Saint George! How is this possible?*

For I came here Nobody, from Nowhere, a fool in a soup-kettle helmet. And now after two short seasons of learnings and adventures, I am to be knighted! A few moments, and I will be truly, rightfully, Sir Percival of the Round Table.

Pure astonishment assailed him.

Eyes on the King, he hardly saw the faces he passed. But one small lady on the right, gowned in red-embroidered blue, drew the corner of his eye. *That one looks familiar.*

He passed and forgot her.

Power punched the small of his back like a treacherous fist. He faltered and almost missed a step.

Then, beautifully, the Power moved through him.

What ailed me before? This is right, this is perfect; doubt, now, at this high moment, would be sin!

They were come to the first step below the King. *Lo, how he shines!*

Another moment, and he will knight me.

This is the King I will follow faithfully, worship, die for. For him I came out of the forest. For him I will find the Holy Grail and place it out of his reach, for it might harm him.

The sun itself seems to shine from him. Am I seeing his aura, as Lili would?

Now, this one gesture I have dreaded.

But this is not hard. This is easy, because it is right.

Percival knelt on the step below the King.

Arthur raised his sword.

Goddamn! True Knighthood comes down like a falcon, like a harrier—

Down came the sword and rested flat, like a friendly hand, on Percival's right shoulder. Joy burned down Percival's right side.

The sword rose, arced over his head, and descended on his left shoulder

Angel Michael, Saint Hubert, Saint George, let me not faint for joy!

Joy flowed like molton gold through Percival, crown to toe.

From above, Arthur's great voice called out to Percival, to the crowd, to the Kingdom, "Rise, Sir Percival!"

And Sir Percival rose.

There rose around him joyful babble from the crowd; and from somewhere in the back, men's voices joined in song; and a shriek.

Shriek?

"There he ish!" A woman's voice shrilled. "Right there! That'sh the one I told you—"

Song and babble died away.

A man roared, "I demand my rights! I demand my rights now and instantly, from the King!"

Late at night I leave the mages' hut and make my way home through narrow, twisting, ill-smelling streets. I carry no lamp. To my Fey eyes this half-moon darkness is like twilight; and lightless, I am close to invisible to the few quarrelling, drink-fogged Humans I pass. This is as well; for in little Ranna's gown, and at this hour, I might draw those stragglers as a doe draws dogs.

I come home to Percival's chamber in the long barracks behind King's Hall, knowing what I must do, and almost pleased to do it. Almost excited.

Niviene explained to me the "rights" which aggrieved Sir Agrain demanded.

In windy morning light, he told Arthur and the whole of Arthur's Dun that Sir Percival had forced a way into his tent, stolen his goods, and despoiled his food and wife. For this, he must be let kill Sir Percival. He has the right.

Percival shook his golden head. He insisted he had not forced entrance, the tent was open; he agreed that he had eaten and drunk, uninvited, because he was hungry and thirsty. He had removed a coverlet, because he was cold. But he strongly, forcefully, and truly denied despoiling any wife.

(The wife, meantime, kept crying out, pointing at him and fainting behind her concealing veils.)

King Arthur looked gravely from one Knight to the other. I thought any moment he would say, "Well, no great harm's been done. You are both Knights of the Round Table, and good men don't grow in gardens. Embrace now, Good Men, and be friends."

He said, "Noon tomorrow. Tournament Field."

Niviene explained. "He had no choice, Lili. This is the rule in such cases."

"You're saying that crowd that loved to see Percy knighted will now watch him be killed!" (Not if I could get him away this night!)

"Not in cold blood."

"Cold blood?"

"Percy will defend himself. He will win, and kill Sir Agrain."

"And the crowd won't mind that, either."

"Right."

"Why don't I get him out of here. I have some Grand Mushroom in my pouch. I could—"

"He would never, never forgive you." That's true.

"Niviene! I must be sure Percy wins!"

Then Niviene told me how to be sure.

Here I hurry down our street toward our door.

Each of these Knights' chambers opens into the street by its own door. Someone has found ours.

A figure muffled in cloak and veil hesitates before our door. It lifts a hand to the door-string; but at that instant I slip in between hand and door.

"Who are you?" I whisper.

The figure springs backward as though a serpent had risen before her; for it is a she, that I see by pale moonlight. Good thing she does not screech and wake the street!

I whisper again, "Who would wake Sir Percival at this hour? And the night before his fateful combat!"

She lifts a corner of her veil to peer down at me. "I know you . . ." she mutters.

"But I don't know you."

"Oh, you musht! You were there in the crowd when Shir Agrain and I rode up, and I shaid—"

"Ah. Yes. You yelled, 'That's him! That's the one!' Now I know you."

Aha! The Goddess brought this one to me just in time!

She cocks her head, shrugs delicately. "I shaw you there. But I never thought you were . . . with him."

"Hush." I don't want anyone wakened, alerted. If I know Percival, even on this night he lies drunk with sleep, not to be waked but by a lightning strike. But this barracks is a wasp nest, full of chambers. Anyone might hear us.

I take hold of her wrist and draw her out into the street. "Let's find a corner where we can talk." My eyes rove the narrow street.

"Didn't come here to talk . . ." I've heard that before.

Down at the corner is a small ale-shop booth.

I know what you came for, Lady, just in time for me. All I need do now is let you take him.

But first, let me know more about you. For all I know, you carry a Bee Sting in your pocket.

I lead her, captive by her delicate wrist, into the ale-shop booth. We sit down together on a customers' bench. We whisper and murmur. (Sometimes I catch myself finger-talking, as I would do with one of my own folk.)

She says, "You shee, it'sh like this. Shir Pershival came into my tent, Shir Agrain's tent, when he wash away. Shir Agrain wash away. And I wash there."

"I know that."

"Oh, yesh, you heard all that thish morning! Let me go on, then." She wiggles, settling herself more comfortably. "When my Lord came back he found everything eaten and my ringsh gone, and the coverlet gone. And he wash very angry."

"Mmmm?"

"And he shaid, 'What more is gone, Lady?' You know what he meant."

"Mmmm?"

"And he beat me."

"What?"

"Shee, he thought I had lain willingly with Shir Pershival. Only then he wasn't Shir—"

"But you never lay with him at all." Willingly or not.

"No, I shertainly never did! But how do you know that?"

"Why, because I was there."

"You?" She leans closer, studying me through her veil. "Come to think, he had shomeone with him . . . a boy."

"Me. That was me."

"Indeed!" She looks me up and down, down and up. "You aren't a boy now!"

"But you say, he beat you. Why did he do that?"

She clucks softly like a hen. "Well, you know, I belong to him. And he thought I had . . ." It's little Ranna, all over again. I seem to hear her whisper, *"If my father knew . . . (shudder!) What good would I be to him then?"*

What good is this lady to Sir Agrain? Whatever good she had for him, it's lost.

She whispers, "I wouldn't mind if it wash only that one time—"

"Hush!" I grip her wrist again. She falls silent immediately. A good thing, because that regular *thump-thump* around the corner is a detachment of guards, coming this way.

She gasps, "Oh!" And shrinks down on the bench.

"Be still. They won't see us . . ."

I raise a mist of invisibility around us. Coldly it drifts between us and the four men who march past. They swing their lanterns to light alleys and corners, and into our booth. They tramp on, past the barracks and around the next corner.

The lady draws breath and dives straight back into her story. "I wouldn't mind if it wash jusht that one time. One hash to expect that." *One does?* "But he won't believe me. He beatsh me every day. Look."

She draws her veil off her face.

That thin, once-cool face is bruised all down the right side. The right eye is swollen shut. The lower lip hangs flabby, revealing knocked-out teeth.

My stomach drops inside me.

Weakly, I repeat her words. "Every day?"

"That'sh why, when I shaw Shir Pershival with the King, I cried upon him."

"You what?"

"I shrieked, 'That'sh him!' Sho he would fight Shir Agrain, and prove I never lay with him. And then I thought . . ." She lets her veil drop. I am grateful. "I thought, why shouldn't I really do it? He won't believe I was virtuoush. Sho, why be virtuoush?"

Wordless, I shrug.

"Beshides, you know, when Shir Pershival took my ringsh he wash lovely! Shoup-kettle helmet and all, he wash perfectly lovely! I almosht wished then . . . But now he'sh knighted and armed, all right and tidy, why now he'sh a God! A veritable God! And you know, in the dark, he won't shee me. He won't notish—"

I draw deep breath. "Listen," I say, stemming her flood of words. "He's mine. You can't have him. I won't let you." *Why not? It would certainly simplify my task!* "But we can stop these beatings."

"We can?"

"Like this."

On the spot, I invent a short spell. *"Devil take your arms, my Lord, cut your hands off like a sword!"*

"Holy Mother! If I shaid that—"

"Not aloud. You only have to think it. And mean it." But has this lady the Power to actualize thought?

"A charm will strengthen it . . . Wait, I must have something here . . ." I'm feeling in my pouch. Knife, handy thong, herbs . . .

I don't carry much in the way of material magic; my magic is in my head, safe from harm and loss . . . Aha! This light, soft touch tingles fingers and soul. I draw out . . . Percival's teal feather!

He picked it up from the snow grail, itself a natural, melting charm, and gave it to me for safekeeping.

He has not asked for it back. Too soft, too airy for his keen purpose, it has melted right out of his mind.

"Here. Keep this safe, but within reach. Hold it when you say your spell."

"Thish little feather?" Behind the veil, the bruised eyes boggle.

"Thish little feather will add weight to your Power."

"Power?" With a light breath she ruffles the feather.

Briefly, my Spirit touches hers. Bounces off hers. Convinced, I tell her, "You have more Power than you think. Look at you! What other lady in this dun would wander these dark streets alone, without a lantern?"

A grin flashes behind the veil. "You!"

"Ah. But then, I'm no lady."

I leave her. One moment I sit beside her, thigh to thigh. Next moment I am gone. Let her ponder that. Then let her leave my Percival alone, and keep her magic feather tenderly. It's all I can give her.

Percival sleeps in our wide, warm bed. On the bed-side chest the lamp still burns. His green-blue aura wafts about him, gentle as his sleeping breath.

I sink down on the bed and study him—my new Knight, my old friend.

What does the Goddess think of Percival?

If I were She, Lady of Life, Percival would be my favorite son!

Bright and big he is, it's true; impossible to hide;

heavy-footed as his great, red horse. But strong! From the deep insides of him gushes a magic fountain of strength, ever renewed. That lady called him "a veritable God." And such he is, to Humans. What need has a God to hide, vanish and sneak like a Fey?

We misjudged our Percy, back in the forest. *"You can't go fishing with him . . . the fish think his hair is the sun, and hide away."* We judged him as one of us . . . which he never was.

As I protected him then, so I would protect him now.

Morning comes soon, and the combat.

If he would use Bee String, his favorite weapon, Percy would win for sure. But he has not carried Bee Sting since we came here to Arthur's Dun. Says it's not a knightly weapon.

Look how far he has come, from his forest oak-nest to this hard-won bed! From Alanna's soup-kettle helmet to the red armor carefully stacked in the corner. He must not stop now, cut down by a vicious, undeserved fury! By a cruel, knighted fool!

My Percy must win this combat.

After that, we must find that Holy Grail he's after. Then Percy will have fulfilled himself and his Quest.

And if the price for Percy's quest is my own quest, if I must give up my Power so that he can win his Power, then, Lady Goddess, so be it.

I draw Victory up out of my gown. I let her dangle between us, twirl softly, reflect golden light. *Hound on trail . . . wind in sail.*

I pull down the coverlet and lay two gentle, suddenly hungry hands upon my Percy, hands like lightning bolts, charged with the Power of so many nights' imaginings!

My Percy awakes.

Last night, by last lamplight, I lifted Victory from my neck. Lying beside panting Percy, I took up his left hand and pushed the ring firmly onto his third finger. It fit perfectly.

Idly, he raised his hand, looked at the ring with dazed eyes. "What is this?"

"A charm," I told him coolly, as though it mattered little. "Her name is Victory."

He studied her. "Dark, it is. No shine."

"It shines within. Wear it from now on, Percival."

"Oh. Goddamn! You mean, wear it for you?"

"For me?" Curious, I turned my head on the pillow to watch him push Victory around his finger. His new, crimson aura, fading now, expanded with every touch to the ring. Well would Victory serve my victorious Percy! (I suppose my own ringless aura must have shrunk, even as his expanded.)

I asked him, "What good would that do me?"

"So I'd remember you. If we should ever part."

What a fool Human notion! "No, Percival. She is for yourself. To bring you Power."

"Power. Only one kind of Power I want now!" He turned to me, reached for me.

But found me not. I was out of bed, pretending preparations for the morning. "Rest now," I told him, busily fussing in a corner. "You'll need your strength tomorrow."

"You're right, Lili." Thinking of the morrow, he smiled a smile of pure confidence, stretched out comfortably on his back and was instantly asleep.

I looked again on his dear face, newly relaxed, newly warm; and I rejoiced. *Not made of ice now!*

According to Merlin, Percy's Quest should now be almost in his grasp.

My own Heart Quest was probably lost, flickering last, pitiful flames, like this lamp.

Well I knew what I had done. Well I knew what the Goddess had done. She had told me. And She had given me a task. For Her sake I would now have to leave Percival behind, alone; yet not truly alone; for I had given him Victory.

I blew out the light.

Now, this morning, I face a stiff, winter breeze at ringside. A much larger crowd than yesterday's has gathered to watch the combat. Behind me all manner of Humans push and jostle, curse and laugh. Too small to defend my space, I manage to stay in front by dodging, vanishing and reappearing, like a snake in high grass.

Ranna's heavy gown and my "invisible" cloak serve well in this bitter wind. From upwind I smell warm bread and those little honeycakes Percival loves. Sales must be brisk as this breeze, which rushes away honey-smell and crowd-smell!

Men have paced off the combat ring in brown,

snow-speckled grass. They have pushed back the crowd and left the space empty.

Lo, here strides a big Knight into the ring, sword and shield at the ready. Red cuirass and greaves, helmet and shield proclaim him my Percival. A murmur of appreciation runs through the crowd. And the crowd does not even glimpse his wide, orange aura edged in red! I see it almost clearly in windy grey light.

Sir Agrain comes in from the other side. His shield is half blue, half orange. His small, dark red aura clings close. Smaller than Percival, he must be far better practiced with the sword. He stands well away from Percival.

The crowd's murmur rises a notch. Some of these same folk watched my Percival knighted yesterday. Then they waited in awed, reverent silence. Merry, now, they wait to see him kill or be killed.

Across the ring last night's bruised lady, heavily veiled, droops near Agrain's handful of men. I wonder what happened to her last night. Did she not use the teal feather?

Horns blow. King Arthur and the Queen approach through the parting crowd. Close behind them come Lancelot and Gawain. Their four mingled auras rise straight and high above the crowd, bright smoke on a brisk day.

Servants place cushioned benches in the front row. The haughty four seat themselves and spread their embroidered cloaks.

In the center of the ring a herald blows a horn,

then shouts into wind and crowd-chatter. Only the combatants on each side of him can hear his words. I think he tells them combat rules.

Once more he lifts and blows his horn.

And now the crowd hushes.

The herald steps nimbly away. For the first time the combatants face each other. Swords *screech* out of scabbards.

Agrain lifts and lowers his sword like a signal to Percival. Quickly, Percival lifts and lowers his sword.

The crowd stands almost silent, with only a rustle here, a mutter there.

Percival and Agrain raise swords and shields, lift feet and come at each other, swinging.

On his gloved finger, Percival wears Victory. *Wind in sail . . .* His heart is hot, no ice crumb left there. Should he stumble; should Agrain's practiced skill begin to weaken him, here I stand ready, spell on tongue, Power gathered in clenched fists. I came here to see Percival victorious, and this I will see.

Swords clang on shields.

Agrain's bloodred aura expands.

The Knights circle each other like fighting dogs. They advance, retreat, strike, ward, high, low, left, right.

Agrain's red aura fills the great circle.

Should I cast a spell?

Contained Power shakes my fists at my sides.

Truly, I am not sure that red aura is all Agrain's. Percival's aura has reddened as well; and now the two auras writhe together, attack and retreat in air, like the Knights below them.

Percival wears Victory.

I need to know if he can win alone, with only her help.

Because I must leave him.

I clasp Powered hands tightly under my chin. Bite my tongue, that wants to shout the spell.

Blow upon ringing blow, Agrain beats Percival back.

A small moan runs through the crowd, as a small thought may run through a distracted mind. Percival is the crowd's man—at least while he still swings a sword.

Back and back he steps, back he bends beneath steady blows. Now he could stumble.

My fists fly up before me, ready to open, to cast forth Power upon Percival. My mouth opens to cry out Power.

But wait! Wait till he actually stumbles. See if he can— Gods!

In the air Agrain's aura swoops toward Percival's.

On the ground, Agrain swoops toward Percival. And overreaches.

Percival has led him on!

Agrain stumbles.

Percival regains balance with one easy step. His sword plunges in under Agrain's cuirass.

A moment the two figures hang there, Percival holding the spit on which Agrain writhes.

Percival yanks out the sword.

Agrain reels toward Percival. Crashes on his knees. Rolls prone on earth.

Midair, his aura freezes. It turns purple, brown, black. It collapses upon him like a huge black veil tossed over a corpse.

Across the circle, one high shriek rends air. The veiled lady faints into the arms of Agrain's nearest man. *In her slippers, I would not shriek and faint! I would sing praises to all Gods. But—to think Human—Sir Agrain must have been of some use to her, and now that use is lost.*

The King rises from his bench. He raises, then lowers, a commanding hand. The rules say Percival is in command.

Agrain's black aura-veil shudders and ripples as though windblown. The man is not dead yet.

The crowd roars.

Percy, make speed! This enemy viper must trail you no more. Another time, he might strike without warning.

Percival steps forward. Raises sword.

His aura that has filled the circle comes rushing back to him. From red, it fades to orange. A wide green border circles the orange and moves inward.

Percival sheathes his sword.

"Why did you not kill him?"

"Lili, I don't know why!"

"You know. You don't want to look at why."

Percival sighed.

"Look at why, and tell me."

A deeper sigh. "Lili, he was breathing."

"So."

"I did not want to stop him breathing."

"Why?"

"Well . . . you know, good men don't grow in gardens."

"This was not a good man! But you could not know that."

"What did you know of him?"

"I saw his bloodred aura. Big as the combat circle! I saw his wife's face." Lili paused, thinking. Then she said, "You realize he may come after you again."

"Nay. He will die."

No doubt of that. The healer who could save him lives not in this world.

"Then you might have done better to stop him breathing then and there."

If every breath he draws this moment is an agony. "Yes. I might have. But why do we argue, Lili?"

"I seek to understand you."

"Now is our last chance to play our new game, alone, in a soft bed."

"Last chance? What last chance?"

Lo! I have surprised her! "We leave in the morning."

"What?"

Percival pulled off his tunic, dropped it on the floor and jumped into bed beside Lili. He left the lamp burning. He wanted to see her face when he delighted her. "So let us spend this time well, Lili, as you have shown me how."

He grabbed for her. Hastily, she sat away up and curled herself small.

"Where are you going in the morning?"

"First light, we pack up and ride out with Lancelot and Gawain!" Percival could hear, himself, how rich satisfaction darkened his voice.

"Where and why?"

"To quest for the Holy Grail. What else?"

"Now? In dead winter?"

"In the spring, the whole Round Table will go questing. Except that we will be back by then, grail in hand!"

"Hmm. Grail in whose hand?"

"Why, in ours!"

"Give that some thought, Percival."

Percival laughed. "You talk like a Human, Lili!"

"I am learning."

"But truly! We are now three brothers. I never had brothers before—except the dead. Now I have Lancelot and Gawain, and I stand by them and they stand by me, and I will hear no word against them!"

"Not from me, no."

"Nor no one else! We three are Arthur's Best Knights. So, as I said, this is our last chance in bed—"

Lili hiked her curled-up self farther away. "Very well; first light, you ride out. As for me, I go another way."

"*What?*" Astonishment froze Percival, eager arms thrown out, at half jump. "What?"

"You think I'll help you find the grail so you can wed Lord Gahart's daughter."

"Aye! And inherit his lands!"

"Nothing in that for me."

"Ah? Oh! Aha! Lili, you are Fey! This wedding game is not for you!"

"No. And neither are you, Sir Percival. From now on."

Lili rolled off the bed entirely, pulled off the top coverlet and spread it on the floor.

Women! A good thing we men don't have to understand them.

But this was certainly disappointing. Now that at last his body had learned ecstasy!

Lili blew out the feeble lamp. He heard nothing more but her sigh of happy contentment as she lay down on the floor.

He relaxed against the pillows. But his eyes would not shut. The darkness showed him sunny-bright pictures of himself grooming the red charger, trapping and dressing hares, starting fires with flint and tinder. Doing all the boring, dull tasks that Lili did.

After while he asked into darkness, "Where will you go, yourself? Now, in dead winter?"

"Me, I'm going home."

"Home?"

"To the forest. Where else? I'm dead tired of traipsing about this Kingdom as your servant boy. This life is too rough for me. I'm going home."

"But . . . It's too far, Lili." *Especially in winter.*

"A four-day ride, if you know the way."

"You don't know the way. And you can't travel alone! Even with all your talents—"

"I'll go with the mages. In a few days."

"The mages . . . Niviene and Merlin? Ah. Well." *Not much danger there. Those two can freeze bandits or Saxons in their tracks, turn aside snowstorms, call hares to their cookfire.*

Still. Funny, cold feeling in the stomach. "Goddamn! I don't like this, Lili."

Down on the floor, Lili chuckled. "Will you miss me?"

"What do you mean?"

"Will your heart hurt for me?"

"No!" *Fool talk!*

Slyly. "But you will miss my talents, Percival."

To be honest . . . "Maybe."

"You'll miss my hunting, cooking, spying. Who will keep the women off you now?"

"Women?"

"You know not how I have served you! They'll eat you up."

Is this a frightening thought? Or is it cheering?

"And my spells. Gods, how you'll miss my spells!"

"Spells?" *What does the girl mean now?*

"Surely you don't think you won all those fights by yourself?"

"What?"

Percival leaped bolt upright.

"Think, Percy! How could you, a fool beggar straight out of a Fey Forest, kill the Red Knight?"

"You saw how! With my Bee Sting—"

"Which I prepared for you. And worked a spell on the spot."

"That may be. But I myself—"

"How could you, who never held a cudgel, beat Lord Gahart's best cudgel man?"

"Why—"

"You who had barely learned to handle a lance, how could you unhorse Sir Cai all by yourself? And I mention not Sir Lancelot, Arthur's Best Knight?"

Percival ground his teeth. The cold hollow that had opened in his stomach was swallowed up in hot rage. "Don't you try to steal my glory, girl! You, who were not even there! You were cooking, back in camp—"

"So you thought. In truth, I was out hunting what to cook. I saw those Knights approach; and I sent you all the strength in the Lady's Victory ring."

"Ring? Victory ring? You mean, this ring? I work no magic! I win by main strength and spirit! I'll have your ring off!"—

Tear it off. Twist it, rub it, rip it off

"Better hold on to that ring, Sir Percival. This morning she defeated Sir Agrain."

"Goddamn! Saint George! I myself, me, Sir Percival, I defeated Sir Agrain!"

"With Victory on your finger. Remember?"

Off with the damned thing! "Take back your damned ring!"

"Percival, I gave you that ring in friendship. Would you throw away my friendship?"

There, it's off. "Fey Witch! Succubus! Here's your ring back, and your evil friendship!" And Percival hurled Victory out into the dark.

I've been here before.

This mist I've seen before, rolling around even the nearest trees.

This lumpy, rough ground . . . I've swung over it before. I've felt Bee Sting thump thigh; I've felt the jar in knees and ankles as I stride forward . . . always forward . . . in haste to go there . . .

I know what comes next.

Aye. There it shows. Dark on the ground.

As before, the stretcher laid before him breaks Percival's stride.

On the stretcher lies a big blond man, naked within his fishing-net wraps. Perfectly still he lies on his back, gripping a fishing spear in helpless hands. He looks up at Percival calmly, though anguish darkens his gaze.

Between his thighs he bears a grievous, bloody wound.

The Fisher King. Won't look!

But Percival has to look at the dreadful wound. He shudders through his whole body. And looks away.

Good for me, it's not my hurt!

But when it is . . . if ever . . . I'll bear it as he does.

Now, I'm going. There. With all good speed.

Percival moves to step over the impassive Fisher King.

Nay. This way.

He steps around the head of the stretcher.

And strides on through mist, over rough ground.

Niviene says, "Lili can start the fire."

Merlin shrugs. "Lili needs not prove herself to me."

But Niviene sits back on her heels by the little tent of sticks we have circled with stones and glints up at me. "Fire-starting was one of the first magics I learned. Let me see you do it."

Despite many tries, I have never yet made fire.

Niviene will not be denied. I kneel down by the sticks and rub my hands smartly, palm to palm.

We will rest in this cold thicket overnight. Gods be thanked there is no snow. Earth sleeps bare, brown and hard. Night comes on.

A few paces away, across a patch of bracken, a small camp spreads along a river ford. Makeshift cabins and tents house the raggedest, saddest Humans I have yet seen. Everyone lurching among the tents limps, or taps his way with a long cane, or bends double as though loaded like a donkey.

I did not want to stop near these folk; their diseases, vermin and griefs may catch us here.

"They are but beggars," Merlin told me, firmly unloading our hobbled ponies, "And some sick. This place is called Swineford, where swine are driven through the ford to market. These folk beg from the drivers, or rob them."

Niviene said, "We've camped here before. The bracken hides us. The beggars don't bother us, for we have nothing."

I nodded toward the ponies.

"Those harnesses bear the King's stamp. They don't touch those ponies."

"But their illnesses may come and catch us."

"Not through the Power Circle I have laid down,"
Merlin assured me.

Very well. I trust Merlin.

Now let me try this difficult art once more.

I lay my warmed-up hands to the tinder under the
sticks and murmur the fire spell.

My hands feel hot. I've never come this far before.

Heat hurts my hands. This time, could I succeed?

Fervently, I repeat and repeat the spell.

Smoke puffs between my fingers! I lift my hands,
and sparks fly up. Sparks. Fly. Up!

A brisk wind blowing to us from the camp carries
away my sparks.

Merlin, standing over Niviene and me, spreads his
cloak between wind and tinder.

Niviene remarks, "It needs more Power, Lili. More
Power." I glance across at her. Through deep dusk,
my Fey eyes catch hers twinkling.

Over at the camp, someone shrieks.

"There," says Niviene, "it's caught." Our little fire
licks up like a new-hatched serpent standing on his
tail. "Oh you of little faith! You didn't even believe
you could do it."

I? I did this?

Unbelieving, I stare down at my little, rising flame.

From the dark, a pony shrills.

Over at the camp, a great voice booms.

Humans cry, scream and babble.

Merlin turns around to look. "Fire," he says,
simply.

Niviene and I stand up and look out over the brown bracken.

The tumbledown cabin nearest us has burst into flame.

This fire must have started by magic. In one moment it has engulfed the whole tiny cabin. Already, streams of fire lick along the wind toward our bracken.

Over the fire-roar and the Human cries, we hear soul-shrinking screams from inside the burning cabin.

I look to Niviene. "Stop the fire!"

"Too strong for me."

"But it's coming right for us! Stop it coming!"

"Oh, aye," Merlin assures me. "We can turn those little flames."

He and Niviene raise their arms to the dark sky and chant spells. I know those spells. But my arms refuse to rise, my throat constricts. Something pounds in my chest as our three panicked ponies hobble away, neighing.

The wind, which blew fire toward us, shifts away northward.

Holy Goddess! What are those beggar folk doing?

Fast as they can, hobbling like our ponies, they run toward the burning cabin. Toward it. Not away.

Women beat at creeping flames with brooms. Men rush to the ford with pails. A line forms, handing full pails of water toward the fire. Too small. And much too late.

I ask the mages, "What are they doing?" But they only chant louder, waving magic gestures at the sky.

By all Gods! A man, surprisingly big and strong, charges into the fire.

"Lady Goddess, he's crazed!"

A small, crippled man follows him into the fire.

Is that what a Human Heart will do?

I snatch Victory up out of my tunic on her thong, and point her toward the fire. My stopped throat croaks out fire-dousing spells.

The big man staggers out of the fire. A small child lies over his shoulders, lamb snatched from wolf. He dumps the child and rushes back into the fire.

I see only fire, hear only fire-roar. Victory points, trembling in my hands. Voice chants. The fire seems . . . the fire seems to stand still.

Out reels the strong man again. With one hand he hauls a woman, hair and tunic on fire. With the other hand he drags the lame man, who drags another child.

I wave. I chant.

The first pail of water arrives up the line, hand to hand, and is hurled over the burning woman.

The fire shrinks. Lowers its voice. But riverlets of fire still burn toward other cabins and tents.

More pails arrive.

With a stupendous crash the hut falls in like a tent of sticks.

(At the same moment, the little tent of tinder at our feet falls in.)

The fire rears up once more, then dies away down. Its roar sinks to rumble and crackle.

The crowd mumurs.

"Hush," says Merlin to me. "Shut it up! You've done it." I didn't know I was still chanting spells.

He grabs me around the waist and drags me backward into dark woods.

I'm on the ground. Merlin kneels beside me, holds me in his arms.

Niviene comes to us silent, with no rustle or footfall. She kneels with us. "No one noticed," she murmurs. "They were all looking the other way."

"Good," Merlin says shortly.

I'm looking up through darkness into their two, solemn faces. I sense other faces behind theirs, up there in the cold dark. I seem to drift, invisible, among these other invisible faces, looking down on us three.

Niviene says, "You doused our little fire too, Lili. We'll leave it dark. No need to attract attention."

Merlin chuckles. "Did those folk out there know what you'd done, they might rebuild the fire and throw you in!"

Gods. "Why?"

"They fear magic."

"Even good magic . . ."

Slowly, I sink back down into the exhausted body in Merlin's arms.

Niviene leans close. "Lili, how did you douse that fire?"

"Don't know."

"Why did you douse that fire? It no longer threatened us. Merlin and I had turned it away."

"Don't know."

I strain to sit up. Merlin lifts me, cushions my head on his sharp old shoulder. Back hurts. Head hurts. Arms hang down all helpless. An awful thirst grips my throat.

Merlin says, "I suspect you started both fires, Lili."

"But I never . . . never before . . ."

"Your power has gone beyond you. Out of control."

One thing I know. "Don't want more Power. No more Power! Don't want Human Heart." That wild, crazifying thing sent men charging into fire!

Niviene laughs softly. "Too late, Lili. Your Human Heart has caught you. Like plague."

The small hoofprints I have followed hungrily through new snow, under evergreens, across clearings, glow fresh in late light.

I pause in my tracks, fingers on Bee Sting. My prey must be very close.

To my right, West River gurgles around ice.

Slowly, step by step, I followed the glowing tracks into a trodden snow trail, and up away from the river. Ahead, I smell panting heat!

Up a steep trodden track I scramble, almost too fast, almost too eager.

Near the top I lie down and inch my eyes up over the rim.

And look straight into golden eyes.

Breath puffs between us.

At first I see only eyes. Then the prey moves, twitches an ear, turns her smooth head, and I see her plain—a small, white fallow doe, invisible in white snow. She stands in the track, head high, looking back at me. She flicks her tail and takes a step away.

Bee Sting comes up, ready between fingers.

But wait.

White fallow doe. Just such a one led the Lady and me into Counsel Oak's shadow once, where I received and rejected good counsel.

Just such a one swam out past Percy and me as we rode our coracle toward the Kingdom. *Turn back,* she signaled. But I misunderstood her.

How many snow-white deer may there be in this forest?

This may well be the same one as twice before.

She looks back at me, flicks tail again, steps forward again.

I push Bee Sting back into belt. I rise up out of snow and follow her.

She takes the straight, trodden track as a Human would. Come to think, (despite hunger, weariness and chill,) this is a Human kind of track.

I am guided.

Mary's Clearing opens before me.

My guide steps aside among snow-laden young pines and vanishes.

Ahead, Mary's bower stands humped under snow. Alanna stands humped before it, reed broom in hand. Brushed-off snow lies flung to both sides, but Mary is still invisible under snow. I am glad.

Walking up gently, I hear Alanna pant and mumble.

Standing close I notice how she has aged. Her braid is white, shoulders hunched and shrunk. In this light I cannot see her aura; but I feel it small, close to her figure, grey.

Softly, I snap my fingers. Alanna's hearing is sharp as ever. She turns to me, peers at me. A moment, and she knows me.

"Little Lili? It is you!"

Little Lili; like little Ranna. *This is how Alanna sees me?*

"I thought you went away with Percy."

"I did so, Alanna." *"Little" must refer to my height.*

"Ah. And now you're back."

"Here I am." *And Alanna knew me truly little.*

Grey eyes widen. "Percy's back!"

I feel her invisible aura expand and swallow me. She drops the broom and dances herself around, awkward as a captive bear I once saw forced to dance in Gahart's Hall. Her gaze sweeps around, past and over me. "Where is Percy?" She cries, "Percy!"

I tell he, "Percy isn't here."

She quiets. "Where?"

"Out in the Kingdom."

"Dead."

"Oh, no! Very alive. He's a Knight of the Round Table, Alanna. Questing the Holy Grail."

"What! What?"

"The Holy Grail."

I feel Alanna's aura crumble. Fast as it expanded, now it shrinks away to a black veil over her face. I remember Sir Agrain's dying aura.

She murmurs, "The Holy Grail. Knights go after that, they never come back. Never seen again. Or if they are seen, they drool and dream. Mad as sick wolves.

"The Holy Grail" she says. "Percy will never come back . . . Before, there was hope . . . but now . . . Now I might as well . . ."

Alanna pulls a good, sharp knife from her belt and punches it into her left breast.

What I should do now; I should turn and go away.

If Alanna wants to die, that's her decision. No right to interfere.

The knife is good and sharp, but it doesn't go far in.

Alanna yanks it out. Shudders deeply. Bleeds a bit. Holds up her left hand and sets knife to wrist.

What I do is, I reach and grab Alanna's right wrist. Take the knife away. Throw it aside.

Now I throw my arms wide and high and close them, almost, about Alanna's waist. We reel together off-balance, and collapse in the snow. Alanna's arms come around my shoulders. Her warmth enfolds me. Her tears drench my cheek. Alanna's tears, Alanna's grief, catch me like plague. I cry, myself.

For Alanna spoke truth. Percival will not come back.

Afterwhile, when both our tears have slowed, I

whisper in Alanna's ear what the Goddess told me the night before the combat. "That's why I came back."

Alanna sits up straight. She dries her eyes on her poor old gown. (Now I know how poor it is!) She staunches her wound with it. She says, "Then I must live."

"Me too."

"We have work to do."

I dry my own strange tears on my tunic. I ask her, "What has happened here? Where is Ivie?"

"Ivie? Oh, Ivie. Her time came, to bear her child, and she disappeared."

Aha. In Fey fashion, Ivie hid herself away, alone with the Goddess, and her child. If she has not been seen since, she is most likely dead.

"I would have helped," Alanna says sadly. "I would have cared for her and the child. But she went away. Ivie turned Fey, and Sir Edik turned Human."

What? "Sir Edik was always Human."

"Only half."

"Sir Edik is half-Fey?" Come to think, I should have guessed that. His small stature, his skills . . . he always finger-talked with the best. So he turned to his Fey half, and tried to forget the other. And now? Alanna means, now he has turned back to his Human Heart. "How has he turned Human, Alanna?"

"He . . . I . . . We are wed."

"Wed!"

"Aye. I would never lie with him otherwise."

"But wedding needs a priest! Witnesses!"

"Not so. True wedding needs only a promise. Holy Mary witnessed ours."

I learn more about the Kingdom, even here!

"A good thing you stopped me just now, Lili. No matter my pain, I had no right to leave my dear husband alone."

Husband!

This is what the Human Heart leads to! Obligations. Rights and counter-rights. Now poor Alanna has not even the right to die!

Merlin warned me that the Human Heart may be its own price. Counsel Oak warned me. *A price is paid for every quest.*

Still embraced, we kneel up together.

Alanna murmurs, "And now, Lili, I have no right to leave you alone, either."

Something moves in my breast, in the area where Alanna tried to stab herself. Something in there opens like a flower, but suddenly—as if spring came and sun shone and flower bloomed all in a moment.

Astonished, I hear myself say, "I won't leave you alone, either."

Alanna lets out a soft cry. "Holy Mary!"

Embraced together, we turn to Mary.

Mary has melted away Her disguising mantle of snow. She stands clear and distinct. Sun glows on faded paint. Hollow wooden eyes watch us.

Alanna breathes, "Miracle!" She knows how much snow was still there to sweep away.

But she does not even see Mary's steady lightning spread through the whole clearing.

Last time I saw this lightning I scrambled down yonder yew tree and fled away.

It holds no terror for me now. Mary's wooden gaze holds no terror.

I only bow my head to Her in solemn greeting, as Ivie used to do, passing back and forth with wood or water.

GODDESS COUNSEL

Green soldier lifts a shining shield,
Golden gleam in clouded field;
  Sun in green grass.
Gold shield becomes a mist of light
That glows alive; a gleaming white
  Cloud in green grass.
Wind tears and bears away white cloud.
Green soldier shrinks in leafy shroud,
  Gone from green grass.
In distant days and distant fields
Will gleam and glow a thousand shields;
  Suns in green grass.

6

Knight of the Quest

"Nay!" Gawain shouted, "I told you! It is the vessel of the Last Supper!

"And I tell you," Lancelot repeated almost patiently, "it is the vessel that held Christ's blood from the Cross—"

"Might could be both," Percival pointed out. He stood a little apart, looking down over the spring countryside spread all green below.

Newly awakened, the three hungry, unarmed Knights had been rolling up cloaks and packing saddlebags when this dispute broke out. Lancelot's Fey Mell had gone scouting for food. Percival remarked sourly to himself that the Fey made by far the most useful travel companions.

Gawain turned on him. "And you, Percival? What did you say it was?"

Percival shrugged. "A magic vessel. It brings forth honeycakes and other food, according to—"

Lancelot snatched up a stick by his feet and broke it in two. "Magic! By St. George! I haven't quested through the winter for any magic—"

"You haven't quested at all," Gawain broke in. "You've drifted along in a royal dream of—"

Lancelot swung half his stick at Gawain's head.

Gawain ducked and sprang on Lancelot.

Lancelot beat Gawain's sides with both sticks.

"Here!" Percival dived in between them. Lancelot cudgeled, Gawain wrestled him. "Hey!" He gasped as they crashed to earth in a flailing pyramid. "Ho!" As they rolled halfway down hill. "Hey-ho!" As they lay in a panting heap.

Percival opened squinting eyes.

Boots stood before his nose. Looking up the boots, he found Fey Mell smiling down, close-mouthed. Over one shoulder Mell held a bulging sack.

"Food!" Percival pushed a knee off his chest and sat up. "Here is our magic grail, Sirs. Bringing forth food according to our desires."

The other two sat up and disentangled.

Softly, Mell remarked, "Hungry man, angry man."

"Man?" Lancelot rose to his knees. "Me, I turned back into a boy!"

"What came over us?" Gawain wondered, standing up shakily.

"Starvation," Lancelot decided. "Show us your wares, Mell. We'll talk later, on full stomachs."

Later, last crumb and scrap devoured on the hilltop, they talked.

Gawain said, "Seems to me we're questing for three different things."

Percival: "Which we don't even know what they

are. Could be a cup, a dish, a bowl. Supposed to be made of gold—''

Gawain: "But from what I've heard of Our Lord, His life, more likely is horn or wood."

Mell finger-talked to Lancelot. Percival watched and understood, more or less.

"Oh, aye." Sadly, Lancelot translated. "If the grail is magic, we each have an equal chance to find it. But if it is holy; if it has to do with Our Lord the Christ, then I'm out of the running."

Gawain admitted, "I'd thought of that."

Percival had not. "Why?" He asked his friend. "Why are you out of the running?"

Gawain and Lancelot looked away, downhill. Mell signed to Percival, *Queen.*

Queen. Gwenevere. Sin. Oh, aye.

A short silence fell among them, which Lancelot broke. "You might do better without me."

Gawain said, "Could be, we'd do better each alone. Each on his own merits."

Percival nodded. All winter an uneasiness had followed him like a cold shadow. What would his companions say if they knew *why* he sought the Holy Grail? Keeping this secret had taught him something about Humanity. He had learned some caution, suspicion, judgment, to keep some distance between himself and his close friends. If he himself kept such a secret, why, maybe they kept their own secrets!

He asked Lancelot, "But why did you come on this quest at all?" *This long, deprived, winter quest!* "You thought the grail was holy from the first."

Lancelot opened his mouth to answer, and closed it.

Mell signed across him to Percival, *Find grail. Prove no sin.*

Goddamn!

In high, stiff language, Lancelot proclaimed their silent decision. "Let us now ride apart, questing each his own Holy Grail. But swear we now brotherhood forever, together or apart."

And so it came to pass.

Percival rode his red charger downhill and away, baggage behind saddle, sword and lance at side and Bee Sting under belt.

Lili had left it for him. Waking after their quarrel, he had found it in her place on the floor. He knew she had not simply forgotten it. This was her last gift to him, and he treasured it as such. Also, though not at all Knightly, Bee Sting remained his favorite weapon.

Once more, Percival found himself transformed. Before this he had thought his goal reached, only to rise, surprised, to a new height. Now at last, he felt himself truly a questing Knight—totally alone between spring earth and sky, without even Lili's Victory ring to help him!

Now my victories will be all my own! No ring, no spells, no magic, no friends, can steal the glory that will be mine!

Lo, here I am.

Slowly he entered Lord Gahart's known fields. He let the red plod quietly along, gazing about him at fields and fold, herd and plowed earth, wondrously delighted. So might a worthy soul enter Heaven.

> *"Go! Bring me here a golden ring*
> *And set it on his finger.*
> *Put satin slippers on his feet*
> *And bid him bide and linger*
> *The while you kill the fatted calf.*
> *My son was lost; he's found again!*
> *Let harper play, let jester laugh.*
> *My son was dead; he lives again."*

So sang the minstrel in Gahart's Hall; and so was it done for Percival. Robed richly again, ale flagon in hand, he sat at Gahart's right hand while cudgelers, boxers and wrestlers competed; nor was he asked to compete, himself. All these contests he watched intently, squinting against firelight. These were the men he would one day command.

Late at night, a servant escorted him outside the hall to a small wicker bower built in a small pear orchard. Pear blossoms scented the air and drifted down like snowflakes, shadows across the full moon.

The bower contained a wide soft bed, lamp stand, bench and chest. Left alone, Percival laid robe on bench and armor on chest. He blew out the lamp and stretched gratefully, naked, on the bed.

Lili came to him.

"Where have you been?" He asked her, making room in bed.

She slipped in beside, against, and entwined with him. She embraced him and breathed down his neck.

He asked her, "Shall we play our game you showed me?"

Her little fingers tingled his skin. Manhood stirred like a sleepy snake.

But at the same time, "Wait!" Percival caught her hand, held it still. For a long time he had been without Lili, and without the protection of her Powers. Of necessity, his senses had sharpened. Now it was he who whispered, "Someone . . . comes."

Someone breathed outside the bower; someone touched the leather curtain at the entrance.

Fey Lili vanished.

Percival sat bolt upright, dream-dazed eyes wide. His fingers sought wildly across the bed for the Bee Sting he always kept close.

He had left it aside. On bench? On chest?

Someone lifted the leather curtain. Full moonlight shone in the opened space. Dark against silver light, a small, slight figure crept within.

Crept in, besides, pear-blossom scent, and another, overwhelming scent, such a scent as to wake body and render soul unconscious.

Percival sighed relief. *No need for Bee Sting.*

The leather curtain dropped into place, cutting off moonlight. In darkness, a robe rustled as the small person tugged and drew it off. Now her perfume filled the place of air in the bower.

Pale in the dark, she glided to him, bent to him, whispered, "Did I wake you, Sir Percival?"

And Percival remembered Lili's angry words. *Who will keep the women off you? They'll eat you alive.*

Rejoicing, he grabbed the pale, warm figure, pulled her onto the bed, crushed her in arms far too long empty. Rolling with her, he nuzzled a wave of scented hair aside and growled in her ear, "Eat me alive!"

She giggled delightedly. "That I will, Sir!" And fell to.

Not for long were they on the bed. Somehow they found themselves on floor rushes. Sometime later, Percival sat on the bench. The girl came onto his lap. Straining to enter her, for the first time he saw her; long pale hair; childish, honeycake breasts; huge eyes reflecting silver moonlight.

Moonlight?

Percival's hair rose. Manhood fell.

A bear snarled in his ear—one deep, deadly snarl, quickly swallowed.

Moonlight flooded through the entrance where the leather curtain had been ripped away.

Bear-big, clad in a linen nightshirt, Gahart stood over Percival. Moonlight glinted harsh on a sword gripped in his left paw, a dagger in his right.

With a stifled cry the girl slid from Percival's lap to the floor.

"Ruin my girl, will you?" Gahart grunted. "God's teeth! Ruin you!"

He drove the dagger into Percival's naked right shoulder.

But I'm unarmed!

Percival felt the blow impact. He felt warm blood gush, but no pain.

Round Table Knights don't attack—

"You're hound food!" Gahart yanked out the dagger and raised his sword.

The girl knelt up, reached both hands, caught Gahart's sword wrist and hung on.

Percival sprang up and seized Gahart's dagger wrist. For some reason his right arm would not work. With only his weakening left hand he held Gahart's dagger away from his heart.

From the floor the girl muttered, "Father!"

Gahart rumbled, "Him first. You next." He managed to slash Percival's right arm and side. Holding feebly to Gahart's wrist, Percival felt each slash, and warm blood erupt, but no pain.

"Father," the girl said, clearer, "I'll scream."

If Percival had the strength, he would laugh.

Strangely, Gahart stepped back away. Stranger, he gave off stabbing Percival's right side. Wondering, Percival hung on to Gahart's sword wrist with all his fast-ebbing strength.

"Father," she'd said.

Goddamn! Gahart's daughter. Lili told me.

Daughter. Stray words from his new education flashed like lightning through Percival's head. "Sin" . . . "obligation" . . . "duty" . . . "rights." "Daughter."

Holy Michael, I'm in the wrong! He's caught me like a thief in his treasury.

"Father," the girl said, wrestling with Gahart for

control of his sword. "I'll scream. I'll wake them all up. They'll all know. Father, let him go!"

Panting, Gahart turned back to Percival, who still gripped his dagger wrist. "Goddamn you, go! Before—"

Blood flowed warmly down Percival's right side. He muttered, "Arms. Clothes . . ."

"Go. Now."

But. What happens to Ranna? That's her name. Knight of the Round Table must protect the weak. Even the guilty weak?

"I'll go now, Sir. But don't kill her."

"You argue with—"

"I'll scream—"

Once more, this silly threat weakened Gahart. He growled to Percival, "You come back, kill you." His teeth glinted like daggers. "Only way you come back, with Holy Grail."

"I'm going. But don't—"

"I get grail, you get girl. Girl for grail. Get it?"

So. He won't kill her.

Percival glanced at her past Gahart's trembling, thirsty dagger. Face whiter than moonlight. Eyes like empty platters.

She must know her father. Maybe . . . maybe all this has happened before!

Percival gasped, "Sir, I'm letting go. I trust in your word."

"God's balls, man, go!"

Percival let go of Gahart's dagger wrist.

Gahart lost balance and staggered back.

Swift and smooth like a Fey, naked Percival ducked out of the bower into moonlit orchard.

Naked Percival slumped over his horse's neck.

As soon as he escaped from Gahart's sword and dagger, his wounds began to hurt. Percival had little experience with pain, but instinct told him that soon this hurting would cloud his mind and fill his world.

Quickly, while he could still think, he made for the stable where his red charger was stalled. *Thank blessed Mary! If he were out to pasture, I could never catch him.*

He had neither strength nor time to saddle the horse. He bridled and led it outside, then climbed up from the mounting block. *Out of here . . . away . . .*

The red was used to spurs and whip. Feeble kicks from naked heels barely moved it along the track. Now and then it would stop and graze; and Percival, fainting into its mane, would wake and kick and haul on the reins till it moved on. *We must be past Gahart's border . . . Pray God we're past his border . . .*

Through the night they plodded, through fields, along forest tracks, past herds and flocks. Percival sank into a sea of pain and dreams. His right side seemed paralyzed. He could not lift that arm. He ached up and down and deep inside. His muscles contracted, bunched and rippled, as if to shake off pain. Now and then blood leaked down his side, warm against shivering skin. He could scarcely breathe for the fire of pain in his ribs.

Light came around them. *Dawn.*

The red stopped; lowered its neck—Percival almost slid down over it—and burbled. Drank.

Water. We're standing in water . . . if I could drink . . . if only I could drink . . . but I'd never get back up here.

Percival hung on to the red's mane, slumped, and dreamed.

He dreamed a dawn-bright lake, reeds, teal and geese flying up in flocks before the charger's wading hoofs.

He dreamed a boat bobbing, not far out in the lake—gaily painted, blue and red; one fisherman, about to toss a net, stood in the boat.

Lili held the red's bridle. *Lili, you're here! When I need you, you're here!*

She waved to the fisherman in the boat.

He sat down, took up oars and turned the boat.

Help. Help coming.

Percival dozed till he heard the boat grind ashore. Feet splashed. A man's voice asked, "What ails you, son?"

Percival almost awoke. The fisherman stood at the charger's head—an old man, grey-bearded. He took hold of the bridle; and strangely, the charger permitted this. Tame as a plow horse, it neither shook head nor arched neck nor stamped warning.

Percival took burning breath to murmur, "She'll tell you . . ."

"Who?"

Fey Lili had disappeared. *As always.*

Barely awake, Percival stared down into a familiar face. Calm. Concerned. Kingly.

"What ails you that you ride all bare like this . . ."
Kind grey eyes widened. "Holy saints, you're hurt!
That wound . . . We must get you to the boat."

The old man came around the horse's side and
lifted fatherly arms to help Percival down.

Fatherly arms . . . first ever . . .

Fainting, Percival fell into them.

Strong arms.

They raised and held Percival against a broad,
warm breast. Cool water dribbled between parched
lips. Blessed water! He swallowed, then gulped.
Slowly, the arms laid him down again.

Alanna.

She bent above him, grave and strong. Not weep-
ing, earnestly, she looked him over, and did not
weep.

Strange. *Before, you wept. No reason. Now you weep
not?*

Alanna laid a quieting hand on his good, left
shoulder and murmured, "Sleep, son." He slept.

Later, he felt his left side bathed. Firm, damp pats
cleansed and cooled from shoulder to ankle. He
waited for his right side to burst into pain like fire;
but something held it still, constrained, unmoving,
and dulled pain.

He slit eyes open to see a gold-haired boy child
sponging his left foot: heel, arch, toes, between the
toes. *See how he droops, poor brat! That iron collar too
heavy. Much too heavy. He'll grow crooked.*

Percival's right shoulder ached as though weighed down with iron. He closed his eyes to shut out pain.

While the child dried his foot he asked himself, Who am I?

In and out of darkness, alone and during treatments, he asked himself, *What is that gentle, constant noise? And who am I who hears it?*

Pain diminished; answers rose like fish in the dark pool of his mind.

I am a body in pain. I am a soul in pain. A forest Fey? No. That one's wrong.

I am a . . . Knight. Of the Round Table. Yes.

Aha! Arthur has no better Knight than me, I . . . Percival. Yes.

And that noise in my ears? That street noise. Heard in town streets . . .

Pictures glowed out of darkness. He saw himself all in red, on a great, red horse. He saw a Knight armed all in red, wait for him with drawn sword. *But he only used the hilt on me. He thought I was harmless . . .*

He saw his poisoned dart in the Knight's astonished eye.

Who is this friend I drink with? Richly robed. And I myself, richly robed.

Dark girl. Small, Tender. Sets a ring on my finger. "Victory," she says. "Her name is Victory."

All these things I have lost. Red armor. Drinking companion. Girl. This last loss the heaviest.

I was Arthur's Best Knight. Now I lie here wounded, in pain, (though much less pain than before!) like an ordinary Knight. An ordinary Man.

I am a Man.

And that noise goes on and on! You hear that in streets, near huts, wherever there are men . . .

I am a Man, one of the Human horde. I am made of flesh and muscle, bone and blood, and all of them hurt. I have made other men hurt; and now, goddamn, it's my turn!

My guardian loved and protected me. She's gone. I lost her, and everything else.

What is that chatter? And, Angel Michael! Where am I now?

Percival awoke.

He lay as in bonds, his left side trussed and bandaged, on straw in a small, neat hall. The fire pit in the middle held only glowing embers. *Summertime, it is!*

Sleeping mats and chests stood against wooden walls. A rough table with stools, a settle, a bench, furnished the hall—and in one corner, a small table covered by a tapestry.

Burning lamp. Covered dish. Horn grail. Aha! Mass altar.

A holy man, a Christian hermit, lives here.

Naturally. Who else would save me?

Slowly, Percival turned his head left, toward the source of light. *If I can turn the rest of me . . .*

He managed to roll halfway over toward the light. Herbs crackled and warmth oozed under bandages. *That's salve, I'll be bound. Not blood.*

Summer light poured through great, wide-open

doors. *Like Arthur's doors at King's Hall! And there's the noise, itself . . .*

Hens minced in and out the doors to cleanse their feathers in a sand hollow just inside. "Bathing," they clucked and gurgled contented conversation.

Wondering about that noise kept me here in this world!

Beyond, broad bright water winked in sunlight. In the shallows bobbed a red-and-blue boat. Ashore, spread fishing nets dried.

A shadow moved in the doorway. Clucking hens scampered out of its way as it entered. Percival almost rose on his left elbow.

Mug in hand, the hermit came to his side, a brown-robed, bald greybeard with a familiar face.

"Think you can drink this yourself? I'll hold you up."

Familiar strong arms raised Percival. Sitting up, hurtfully, he held the mug himself.

"My name is Father Fisher," the hermit said in his ear. "Call me 'Father.' "

Resting between sips, Percival croaked, "Have you been caring for me, Father?"

"Cedric and I."

Cedric. "Slave-collar boy?"

"Aye."

"Collar . . . too heavy."

"I can't file it off with these hands." Percival glanced down at the gnarled, swollen hands locked at his waist.

"Thank you, Father." Percival drained the mug. A

new sensation opened like a trapdoor in his gut. "I am hungered!"

"Aha! We've been waiting to hear you say that!"

The first nourishment Cedric brought to Percival was a bowl of white liquid. Thirsty for ale, Percival gazed suspiciously down into the white drink. "What's this?"

Cedric looked surprised. "Milk, Sir."

"Milk? What babes live on?" *Horrible milk that peasants drink.*

"Father says you drink it, Sir."

"Aaargh!" Unwilling, Percival sniffed at the milk. "Ugh!"

"Father says it will heal you."

"Ah?" *Heal me? Then it is medicine. No surprise if it smells cursed.*

"He says, drink that, and you get to eat."

Eat!

Percival lifted and drained the untasty stuff in one decisive motion.

His reward was a smidgen of hard bread with fish. The fish was delectable.

In the following days his meals remained the same—bread, eggs and fish, with herbs. But he received a bite more each time, till at last his wooden trencher arrived full and overflowing. And each time, he was obliged to drain a bowl of milk. He grew used to that.

The first walk Percival took was to the Mass altar in the corner.

He had stood up before, dragged on a patched

linen tunic, and hobbled around his straw bed, with help. This time he rose up and dressed alone. Fixing his gaze on the Mass altar, he set out to reach it.

Father Fisher's hall had been built long ago for gentle living; but now the altar, with its bright vessels and tapestry, was the only touch of wealth and rank left. Percival had lain in bed long enough, wondering at it. Now it offered a goal, an incentive, to move his pain-frozen muscles.

Get close enough to see the tapestry. Then I'll quit.

Left foot, right foot, *ahhhgrrr!* Left foot. Right foot. *Uuuuh!*

Up close, panting, right side aching fiercely, he leaned against the wall.

Just see . . . What I came for . . . Tell Father what I see. Prove I came this far.

Much of the tapestry was hidden under horn grail, covered dish or lamp.

If I could move this stuff . . .

Nay! Christ Himself lives on this altar.

Every morning at sunup, Father Fisher said his Mass here. He broke the rough bread Cedric baked, blessed it and turned it into Christ Himself. Cedric would bring Percival his share, and the three of them partake. What might be left went back into the covered dish. *Goddamn, can't touch that!*

Reverently, then, and painfully, Percival bent to see what he could of the mysterious tapestry.

White fallow deer pranced all along the golden border among flowers larger than themselves.

Look on top. Under the sanctuary lamp.

Under the lamp walked a tall, willowy maiden carrying a . . . *Don't touch the lamp!* . . . a burning candle.

Behind her, mostly under the covered dish *that holds Christ Himself!* a second maiden carried a . . . spear. *Dripping blood, goddamn!*

The blood dripped handily into the huge, gold-thread cup grail held up by a third maiden. *Must be heavy for her as Cedric's collar!* The three moved as in a dance, or procession. Jewels winked thick as snowflakes in their flowing hair and gowns.

Seen it! Can describe it

Percival would have fallen, but hands seized his elbows from behind and held him up.

He gasped, "Didn't touch a thing, Father."

"That's well. Can you make it back to bed like this?"

"Give me your arm . . ."

Safely back on his pillows, Percival asked about the tapestry. "King Arthur has nothing grander in his hall!"

"It's very old. Been in my family for generations."

"Looks new!"

"That's because of the air."

"Air?"

"This is a sacred spot, son. All things do well here. I myself am older than you might think. Anywhere else, my Credric would have died of his injuries. I found him hurt worse than you! Anywhere else, you yourself would have died."

"I know it is your healing Power—"

"Not so much mine, as that in the air. Our holy

air is healing you this moment. Before long you will stand and walk outside with me. By Saint Peter! Before long, I'll take you out in my *Josephus*!"

"*Josephus?*"

"My boat. We'll go fishing!"

True to the father's word, a few days later Percival stepped among fluttering chickens out the great doors and into sunshine.

There stretched the lake, almost as far as he could see. There rocked the blue-and-red boat, *Josephus*, on breezy wavelets. Swan and teal winged windily over reeds. Farther along the shore, a great red horse grazed beside a brown goat. Both animals moved free as the wind, untrammeled by hobbles or halters.

Father Fisher cupped his gnarled hands and honked, "Ru-uu-udy! Ho, Ru-u-u-udy—Oh!"

The red horse lifted its head and looked toward Father Fisher. It turned toward him. *Goddamn! He's coming!* It came at a trot. Close and closer the red horse trotted, earth echoing its hoofbeats. It came up to Father Fisher and dropped its nose into his hands.

"Should have brought some bread for him. Wait for your bread, Rudy. Stand."

Father Fisher went back inside the hall.

Percival stared, unbelieving, at the red charger he had never named, this friendly creature he had never befriended. Rudy looked fatter and calmer now than Percival had ever seen him, although ungroomed.

The brown goat trotted up beside Rudy, full udder swinging.

Father Fisher reappeared, bread for both animals

in his hands. Feeding them, he said to Percival, "Nanny's milk healed you, along with the air."

Nanny. The brown goat gave the medicinal milk Cedric had brought twice a day.

"He thanks you," Father Fisher told the goat. "Though he won't say the words, he thanks you." To Percival he said, "Look out at the island."

Island? Ah, yes. That little smudge out near the middle. Rocks and three trees.

"That is our Holy Isle."

"Holy?"

"As Nanny here gives milk, so Holy Island gives blessed Power. You can see the oaks?"

"I see three trees."

"Oh, to have young eyes! Mine can barely make out the island, itself. Those trees mark a spring of holy water that rises from the depths of the earth. The water flows down three narrow streams into the lake and sanctifies the lake. The lake sanctifies the air around it. This Power is healing you, Son."

Percival drew a deep breath of holy air. Gratefully, painlessly, his lungs took it in. *Something is healing me. Why not this air?*

Lili would believe it. No question.

Percival and Father Fisher rowed close past Holy Isle. Evening light glowed in the lake. Holy Isle's three ancient oaks shone golden.

The father's aged hands could still cast a net, if not mend it. Two nets drifted behind the red-and-blue *Josephus*. Father Fisher rowed slowly, patiently. Percival could not row until his side mended entirely. Meantime, Father Fisher's arms worked harder than his hands. And those arms still retained a quiet strength, a shadow of youthful might.

"Father, what makes the spring on Holy Isle holy?"

Lili would say it was holy because it comes out of Mother Earth. Father Fisher will say something else entirely.

The father rowed slowly. "A druid told me the spring is the Goddess's footprint."

"What do you say, Father?"

"When my ancestor, blessed Joseph of Arimathea came here, he drove his staff into the earth at that spot. Maybe the spring rose up then. Maybe the spring was already here. But his staff sanctified it. My ancestor Joseph sanctified this place."

"He built your hall on the shore?"

"Nay. The hall is no more than a hundred years old. But Joseph's blood has lived here since the time of Our Lord."

"How has your family shrunk so small, Father?"

Sigh. "Daughters wed far away. Sons killed in battle. Children dead. Diseases, mischance. Blessed Joseph has sons enough, but in far places."

"Now at this lake you have Good Folk, instead of relations."

Percival meant this remark to encourage and cheer; but Father Fisher paled, and dropped an oar *splash!* into the lake.

Percival reached after it. Instant pain brought him

up short. The hermit fished it back with the other oar. He shipped both oars in the boat, crossed himself broadly and rested. Holy Island swam slowly away behind them.

"Have no fear, son. This place is far too holy for . . . those you mentioned."

"This morning before Mass I stepped outside. A small, dark girl was bathing downshore. She vanished clean away while I blinked." (Percival had signed to her, as Lili had taught him. Yet she chose to vanish.)

The Father wiped sweat from his brow with the hem of his robe. "Your young strength returns, with all its wants. These wants appear to you as a bathing girl."

"I have few such wants, Father."

"Is that so?"

"They say I am made of ice. But you know, the Good Folk are much cleaner than us Humans. They do love to bathe. And I did see her!"

The Father gurgled politely—not disagreeing, not yielding.

"That is not all. The other day I spied a small brown face under a small brown cap. It watched from under a willow branch as we rowed past. Then it vanished. Now why would I daydream such as that?"

"Believe me, son; we have no such folk here."

"You might be wise to leave bread and milk for them on the doorstone. Or they may rob you."

Father Fisher ground his teeth. "Such would never

dare come so near my altar, and that which sanctifies it!''

Calm him! Be ashamed that you have disturbed him!
''You must be right about that, Father. For they have
not robbed you.''

''Why are you so interested in . . . them?''

Percival hesitated. *Never have I told this to any, even
to my friends.*

*But I can trust the father. If not, where in the world
can I trust?*

''I grew up in a Fey forest, among them. They
should have been my folk. But they rejected me.''

The hermit crossed himself. He leaned forward.
Slowly, he drew the whole story from Percival while
they drifted, their nets dragging heavy behind the
boat.

At last the father decided, ''You need spiritual
counsel more than healing! That must be why God
brought you here to me.''

Percival heaved a sigh like a sob.

''Son.'' The hermit laid a hand on Percival's knee.
''What ails you?''

''Nothing ails me now, Father. Thanks to you.''

''I speak not of your wound, which I know. I speak
of your sorrow. A steady, lasting sorrow, too much
for so young a man.''

I have told him so much already!

Percival looked at evening light fading from the
lake; at a new moon poised over the hall, where Cedric had just lit a small fire to guide them in. *I love
this place.*

I love this man.

He took a deep breath and confessed. "Father, all my life I have looked at the sky. But never once has the sky looked back at me."

With all his age and wisdom, can he understand that?

Father Fisher's troubled face cleared. He leaned back away, took up his oars and bent to row.

"For that, I have a cure."

I knew he would!

"What cure, Father?"

"Midnight tonight. New moon. Pentecost season. We'll do it."

"Do what?"

"The holiest, most sacred healing. The highest act possible to Humankind. Pull the nets closed, Percival, Not even trying, we've caught enough."

Midnight.

Sleepy Cedric and eager Percival waited at the table. Father Fisher brought a white cloth from a chest and spread it on the table. On this he placed a small stoppered bottle and the covered dish from the altar. He left the cover aside, revealing sacred, consecrated bread crumbs within.

What is this, a Midnight Mass?

Back at the altar, Father Fisher hesitated. He bowed deeply, then stretched a hand toward the horn-cup grail.

We've never used that at Mass.

Father Fisher drew back his hand. He stood

contemplating the horn grail. He bowed to it again, and took it up, two-handed.

Cedric yawned aloud and shrugged at his iron collar. Almost, he stretched; but a sharp poke from Percival startled him back awake.

The hermit sat down with them and set the grail in their midst. Raising prayerful hands and eyes he intoned, "Brethren, behold the grail of Christ's Last Supper."

The grail of Christ's Last Supper . . . What did Gawain say?

Shiver.

"This grail stood at Our Lord's right hand when He said, 'This is my blood—' "

Trembling, Percival gulped lumpy spit.

". . . This grail carried the wine that first became His blood—"

Percival could no longer silence himself. "You say this is the Holy Grail itself?"

Pausing in his recital, Father Fisher turned an annoyed face toward Percival. "No, I did not. I said, 'Brethren, behold the grail—' "

"Of the Last Supper! This is the grail for which the Round Table quests! The grail for which *I* quest!"

Father Fisher lowered his hands. They nested protectively around the grail. "Listen, son. My ancestor, blessed Joseph of Arimathea, brought this grail here and handed it down, a sacred trust, to his descendants in this place—of whom I am the last. For I have no son, and Joseph's children are scattered."

"Father!" Percival stammered, "Give this Holy

Grail to me for King Arthur, the greatest king in the world! In his hands it will be safe and venerated."

The hermit sighed. Slowly, loudly, he insisted, "This is not the Holy Grail for which you quest."

"You said, the Last Supper—"

"Holy as it is, this is yet a material, earthly grail, made of humble horn."

"As to that, Arthur will not mind that it is not gold! How could it be gold, if Christ Himself—" Percival had wondered that, before. Certainly, this ancient horn vessel, nearly transparent from wear, totally unadorned, looked nothing like the Holy Grail he had expected.

But then, what did? Lili had pointed out, a "grail" could be a cup, or a dish, or a platter, or a wide bowl. And if Christ had used it on His penniless wanderings, it could hardly be crusted with jewels. Come to think, it would much more likely look—

Firmly, Father Fisher shook his head. His fingers tightened defensively on the base of the grail. "The Holy Grail for which Knights quest will never be found."

"Goddamn! It sits right here on this table—"

"Sir Percival!"

The mild hermit's voice flashed a steel edge. Percival drew back, marveling at himself. Even Cedric jerked awake from his doze and sat up almost straight under his collar.

"We three are gathered here to perform the highest healing service under Heaven, purely for the good of your immortal soul."

Abashed, Percival bowed his head.

More gently, "This grail of the Last Supper is a holy, sacred healing tool, the most powerful in the world. It belongs to Joseph's kin. Sir Percival, look you not upon it with greed, avarice or ambition!"

Percival's trembling hands still twitched uncontrollably toward the grail. He clasped them hard under the table.

"Now. Where was I? I must begin again. Interrupt me not again."

Percival nodded acquiescence.

"And you, Cedric, stay awake. We need your prayers, the prayers of a child. 'Suffer the little children . . .'"

Cedric bobbed on his bench to stay awake.

Father Fisher drew the grail closer to himself, away from Percival. Again he raised prayerful hands and eyes to Heaven. "Brethren, behold the grail of Christ's Last Supper . . ."

Recitation finished, the Pater Noster said, a long poem intoned in Latin, (which Percival was beginning to understand,) the hermit poured ale from the stoppered bottle into the grail.

Cedric made a face, then clapped his hands over to hide it.

Well. This is the first ale I've seen here. Cedric isn't used to it . . .

The father took a pinch of consecrated bread crumbs from the dish, then passed it to Cedric. Cedric took his pinch, and passed the holy vessel to

Percival. Reverently, he consumed the last crumbs and replaced the dish in the center.

The father picked up the grail in both hands and drank. He wiped a slightly soured expression from his mouth with his sleeve, and leaned to present the grail to Cedric's lips . . . and then across to Percival. Firmly held by the hermit's two hands, the Holy Grail approached Percival's lips. *Aaaagfh!* The worst ale Percival had ever smelled or tasted slid down his throat. He nearly made a Cedric-face, himself.

The Holy Grail returned to the table, closer than before to the father's elbow. Father Fisher bowed his head, finished a silent prayer and smiled around the table. "There."

"Are we done, Father?"

"For now."

"But . . . we do this every morning!"

"Now, my son, it is your turn to work holy magic."

Magic?

"It is for you now to sleep, here at this table."

Sleep?

"You will find it easy. The ale was not consecrated; I added an herb to it."

Aaaah. That explains . . . Percival laid arms on table, heavy head on arms. He blinked, and noticed Cedric head to head with him, already asleep.

"Right," said Father Fisher, softly. "Just so. Sleep now. And dream."

MERLIN'S COUNSEL

Wine-sweet, God's own blood filled
A golden grail.
Passed hand to hand, no blood-drop spilled
From that gold grail.
Passed age to age, this mystic wine
Within the grail
Turns each of us a holier shrine
Than golden grail.
Then let us each drink God's own blood
From God's own grail
Though never find, by land nor flood,
The Holy Grail.

7

Knight of the Grail

Mist hung heavy over Holy Isle.

Percival and Cedric sat side by side on the sandy beach of Holy Isle, where never had they set foot before. No footprints led to them through sand. Some huge eagle might have dropped them here, out of the mist. Mist-hid lake waves lapped slowly on nearby shingle.

In a deep voice not his own, (which might be his own in a few years), young Cedric commanded, "Behold."

Golden light flickered and flared through mist. It wobbled, swayed, advanced. Percival made out a tall, burning candle in a tall, golden candlestick. A tall, gold-haired maiden upheld the candlestick. She came close up and stood, gazing down at Percival.

After her a dark-haired maiden bore a lance, heavy on her slender shoulder. Thick red blood dripped from its point. Standing by the candle-bearer, she gazed down at Percival.

Out of the mist, then, stepped the third maiden, whose long hair hung red as flame. She bore a great golden grail that caught the lance-dripped blood. Three abreast, lovely as good fairies, rich-robed as queens, they looked down at Percival; and he noted with some surprise that their three calm faces were the same.

Again, young Cedric's adult voice commanded, "Behold."

At the maidens' feet a stretcher appeared on the sand; and on the stretcher a naked man wrapped in fish nets, and wounded between the thighs. Wound and mouth gaped sadly.

I have seen this before. This is the Fisher King. And lo, I am dreaming.

Percival leaned down to the stretcher. He asked the King, "Sir, what ails you?"

Lost in pain, the King could not answer.

An embroidered hem swept forward. Percival looked up. The flame-haired maiden leaned to him, across the Fisher King. She stretched out both delicate hands, bearing the great golden grail between them. Her silent lips formed the word, Drink!

Percival took the grail from her. *Heavy!* And looked within.

Blood. The great, golden grail brimmed with lance-dripped blood.

The silent word, *Drink!* echoed in his misty head. *Drink blood?*

Revulsed, he held the grail away. *Goddamn! I am no wild beast, Fey or Saxon, to drink blood! No Knight of the Round Table drinks blood!*

Below the extended grail the Fisher King clasped prayerful hands. Above the grail, the flame-haired maiden formed again the silent word, *Drink!* And she pointed down at the Fisher King.

So. This is how to help the King? Drink blood?

> *Upon your way you hear a cry?*
> *Answer it! Help, save or die!*

If I can drink milk, I can drink blood. God's eyes! They could ask more than that! They could ask me to kill a dragon to save him, and I would do it.

Percival clenched and ground his teeth. Roused courage to kill a dragon. And sipped blood.

Heady sweetness rolled on his tongue. *Grace of God! Blood? This is finer ale than Lord Gahart's! Better than what Mage Niviene serves at King's Hall!*

Percival closed happy eyes and drained the Grail.

The heart in his breast opened like a flower. Like a huge red, pulsing flower it burst through bones, flesh and skin. It contained beach and Holy Isle, lake and sky. On his closed eyelids Percival felt hot sunlight. *What happened to the mist?*

Intensely happy, Percival sucked up the last drops of blood and opened his eyes.

Sunshine flooded the beach. Light winked on water, and through the three fast-fading maidens.

The Fisher King smiled up at Percival. His ghastly wound had closed, healed, gone.

Percival looked out at the lake. *I am the lake.*

Looked into the sky. *I am the sky.*

The sky looked back at him.

Calm and grave, the disappearing, flame-haired maiden reached and took back the great golden grail. Maidens and grail vanished like wisps of mist. The Fisher King sat up on his stretcher.

But once again young Cedric commanded, "Behold."

On the lake edge a dark cloud formed and rose high.

Quickly it took on near-solid form. Huge, bare feet rooted in the shallows. Darkly ragged, tall as ancient oak, a stern, heroic giantess looked grimly down upon Percival. In one rough, great hand she held a Bee Sting, still his favorite weapon. It held poisoned darts as long as jousting lances.

Breathless Percival heard his heart beat louder than Flowering Moon drum. Every hair on head and body stood rigid.

After all you've come through, don't be killed sitting down!

Percival scrambled up and faced the giantess. Wildly his hands sought for weapons in his clothes— Bee Sting, sword, dagger, knife—and found none.

His tongue swelled down into his throat.

Goddamn! God's teeth! This is fear.

I never felt it before.

"The Fisher King was yourself."

"Nay, Father, he was yourself!"

"He took my face. Maybe to lead you to me. But his wound was your own."

"Father, I have suffered no wound in my life but what Lord Gahart gave me. And I naked!" (Percival could not put that astonishment behind him.)

"You told me once you were made of ice. You are no longer ice. You have drunk Christ-blood."

"The sky looked back at me . . ."

"So long as the sky sees its own reflection, it will look back at you."

"Father! How shall I hold that reflection?"

"The dark giantess . . . you must deal with her. You know her, what or who she is?"

Shudder.

"You know her face."

Gently, teeth chatter.

"There lies your final quest. To be free you must find and confront her."

Deep sigh.

"What ails you now?"

"Father, I have sinned!"

"Before you go, I will hear your full confession."

"But I had no choice. It was sin or die."

"Before you go. Which may be soon. Your wound looks much better than yesterday."

"But how shall I go, Father? I have nothing in the world, save Rudy." *Not even a Bee Sting.*

"Hah! You will wear my layman's clothes from long ago, and carry my sword and shield."

"Father! You have such?"

"I was not always a hermit. When you have confronted the giantess, come back home."

"Home!"

"I have found a son."

"And I a father! But before I go from here I will file off Cedric's iron collar, no matter what time it takes."

"Amen!"

Three of us spin and card in Lady Villa's sunny courtyard.

Around Lady Villa the apple trees of Avalon hang low,

bowed beneath harvests of small, wizened apples. This moment, I would love to walk beneath their branches! Pick one apple here, one there. Eat one, toss one!

Around Apple Island the Fey lake ripples away to far, forested shores. I could wade in and watch the traveling ducks thunder past. Maybe draw one to me with a spell.

Fishing coracles drift well out, beyond the reach of island magic, or so the fishers hope!

I sense that one of these is just setting out from the western shore, poling vigorously toward us. I could wander out there and look . . .

But nay. This scratchy wool must be carded, now.

All three of us have changed. Small and slender as ever, perched gracefully on the fountain rim, Lady Nimway has taken on a wealth of wrinkles; and her newly knobbly fingers strain at the spindle. But Victory glints in the sun, swung against her green gown; and I feel her aura, (invisible in strong light,) wider than the villa.

Alanna has gained weight and calm. Marriage and acceptance of loss have restored the dignity she must have owned in the Human world. (Wandering out there, I saw Alanna-like ladies. Now I know what she must have been, long before Percival was ever born.) Now, like a serene Goddess she balances beside Nimway, spinning with Human ease.

Heavily pregnant, I sit on the ground a little away, pretending to card wool. Bits of wool fly into eyes and nose, and dust my tunic. After this, I will swim!

The Lady asks me again, "Lili? You are sure my son Lugh gave you no sign? No message to bring back to me?"

Inwardly, I sigh. I have told the Lady, and I have told her . . . On this subject she is as blind, deaf and wishful as any foolish Human!

"Lady, I thought Lancelot's squire Mell was your son Lugh."

Sniff!

"I never looked at Sir Lancelot! If he gave a sign, I did not see it."

Sadly, she smiled down at her spindle.

"And I never dreamed he could be Fey!"

"He is not."

Now, here is something new! "Your son Lugh is Human?"

"Born Human, Lili. Human blood. They say it always tells in the end. But now, Lili, try to remember. Did you ever hear Lancelot say, 'When I was a boy on Apple Island'?"

"Never that I heard."

"Maybe once he said, 'When I go home' . . ."?

"Never, Lady."

We have been through this before. Annoyed, I glance up at Nimway. And I see beyond her sad face. I see into her torn, wounded heart, that thrashes like a slowly dying animal.

Instinct whispers, *Run! Get clear of this grief before it catches you.*

My new Human Heart yearns to share it, to lift a good, sour portion of it from Nimway's bowed shoulders to my own.

Oh, to skip out away from here!

"Lili!" Alanna scolds me lightly. "Do you imagine you are carding wool?"

"Achoo!" (Wool in nose.) "Nay, Alanna. I but play a game, here."

"Whose babe is this wool for, after all? Your own hands should work it! If only a little."

"I am not Human. Work bores me."

"Hah! I'll tell you a secret!" (Which she has told me before.) "Work bores us all. That's how we die in the end, from that boredom. But how else will you wrap your little one?" As if her own work could not wrap all the little ones in the Forest!

"Why, in spiderwebs, Alanna! In cocoon silk!"

My Spirit walks under the apple trees of Avalon. My Spirit wades into the lake and beckons a passing duck. If I were on my feet right now—and free of this gently moving stone in my belly—I would vanish away while the ladies watched their threads!

Alanna glances up at the misty, mellow sky. "My dear husband must be poling across to bring me home by now." So that is the coracle I sensed earlier, making for us. "Dear husband!" That word that so startled Percival is Sir Edik's joy and glory!

Alanna wraps up her work. "Lili, will you look to see if he is coming?"

Very gladly I rise, tumbling my work in a heap. Delighted, I glide away through the dark entrance into open, unwalled sunlight.

Stretching, dancing slowly about on tiptoe, I look out over the lake. Here swim the ducks, geese and swans I sensed from inside the villa walls. There drift the fishing coracles, turning and dipping, dragging full nets. And here comes the one I knew was aiming for the island. Dear Husband, coming to collect Dear Wife.

I step back into the dark entry and signal to Alanna.

Turning, I inspect the approaching coracle again. Maybe it's not Sir Edik after all. Two heads bob in it—one white, one . . . sunny gold.

Sunny gold? On the Fey lake?

Gasp.

My babe within folds up his tiny knees. He gathers all his little force and *kicks* me, square and rough, in the side. *Aaagh!*

When I was young I went questing. That which I sought, I found. Now with new Power I can start fire with bare hands. I can see the secret thoughts of others, and their fates, bright and dark threads woven through their auras. But every day I pay again the high price for this Power. Daily I carry my Human Heart within, heavier than Percival's babe.

This heavy Human Heart expands now in my throat, so I can hardly breathe.

Steadily the coracle draws near. Is it material? Or is it a vision of the future?

Or is it maybe a deceptive, false daydream born of desire? The Gods know there is enough desire loose here on Apple Island to engender such false seeing!

Alanna comes to stand beside me, bundle on shoulder. She shades her eyes, and gasps.

If she sees the coming coracle, the two heads, they are materially there. Alanna sees only material fact.

She draws in one great breath.

"Hush!" I seize her hand just in time to forestall one of her famous screams. This scream of joy would rend lake and sky, send birds up in rolling wing-thunder, and maybe break the good spell that draws the miraculous coracle close and closer.

Alanna lets out her great breath. She dumps her bundle, catches up her gown and *runs*, heavy, stumbling, down to the shore.

Close in the oracle swings around as Sir Edik digs in his pole.

Silent, Alanna wades in.

Silent, Percival heaves himself out into knee-deep water.

Silent, Percy and Alanna wade together and fall, *splash*! to their knees.

Each meant to kneel to the other and beg forgiveness, in the Human way. But falling together, they simply embrace. Fumbling, clutching, straining together, they embrace in silence; forgiven and forgiving.

On his knees in the Fey lake, Percival clasped his giantess. Rough, white hair prickled his face. Strong arms trapped his neck. Breath sobbed warmth into his ear, while the rest of him sopped up lake-chill.

The cold Fey lake washed through Percival. It washed out his empty stomach, stinging wound, swollen heart. It washed out pride, yearning, confusion, the last shreds of anger and never-acknowledged fear.

Cleansed, he strove to rise. But Alanna hung on him, drenched and limp. He had to raise her with him. On the second try he heaved them both halfway up, only to splash back down. His third effort brought them to their feet, dripping and clinging.

Hopefully, he looked over Alanna's shoulder to the only happy landscape of his childhood—Apple Island.

Here he had played with Lili, his only friend, while Alanna and Ivie visited the Lady. He and Lili had built bowers and dens of twigs, and modeled tiny figures from lake mud to live in them. They had learned Mage Merlin's songs at his knee, and sung them, and then made up their own. Here they had netted minnows in the shallows, and shot darts at flitting songbirds. Here, Lili had helped him trap his first hare.

Or had all this been a dream?

Real Apple Island still rose gently from the lake. Loaded apple trees bowed down around lofty Counsel Oak. Lady Villa still gleamed, a little less white, through a few more encircling vines. The shore stretched rocky, autumn-brown.

A brown sapling lifted roots from land.

Graceful as a walking willow it came down to the water.

With no splash or gurgle, Lili stepped into the lake.

Percival's clean-washed heart lurched and beat again.

Coming to him, small feet gliding like fish in the water, Lili shone.

Holy Michael! She always talked about auras. Now I'm seeing one!

Coming to him, smiling, Lili waded through rosy light. Leaving no ripple she came to him.

"Lili, goddamn! You shine so bright!"

GRAIL COUNSEL

Gold rings a center pearly white;
Around the gold, a blue ring bright;
Gold and blue, snow-dappled white.
Around the blue, red ruby light,
This too, snow-dappled pearly white.
Around the red ring, infinite white.
White inside and outside white,
Gold, blue and red, snow-dappled white,
One day will meld, infinite white.